VOLUME ONE

BOOK THREE

THE BATTLE FOR ICEOTH

BY

DWAYNE ANTHONY MADRY

Printed in the United States of America

First Printing, 2024

ISBN 978-1-963089-02-8

Cover Design by JessHavok

www.SAHAEL.com

Intoduction into Sahael

As Oadira reaches the chosen right of election, her birthright as the rightful heir to the Orishan bloodline becomes undeniable. With a powerful presence that commands attention, she asserts her authority and takes her place as the Black Madonna, embodying the legacy of her ancestors and solidifying her position as a formidable leader.

With her newfound status, Oadira unleashes a wave of transformation, instigating a chaos of her own making. She channels her inner strength and taps into the depths of her powers, causing the continent of Iceoth to be thrust into a battlefield of epic proportions. The once peaceful landscape is now a battleground, with forces clashing and energies colliding in a symphony of power and chaos.

The pivotal moment comes when Oadira's actions trigger a profound reaction from the very essence of the world itself. As the horizon meets the waters surrounding Iceoth, a cataclysmic event is set into motion, heralding the second sign foretold in ancient prophecies. The convergence of horizon and water unleashes a cascade of events that reverberate across the land, marking a turning point in the destiny of Oadira and her people.

With the second sign unleashed, Oadira's role as the Black Madonna is further cemented, her power and influence transcending the physical realm as she navigates the turbulent waters of fate and destiny. The battlefield of Iceoth becomes a crucible for her transformation, shaping her journey towards a future filled with challenges, revelations, and ultimate triumph.

CHAPTER CONTENTS

CHAPTER I

WAHANGARA FOREST

Iceoth, Benin Palace

"You're only two centimeters dilated, my queen." Lyshyla whispered as another contraction tightened Oadira's stomach. She held fast to the Marula pole in the center of the birthing chamber, letting the pain subside. Sweat dripped onto her lips, salty and unpleasant.

Back on the Lalaurie estate, Oadira saw numerous births. If she was only two centimeters dilated, it would likely be many hours before her child would be born. She had already been in labor for the past two hours, but progress had been agonizingly slow. She wanted Ozias here with her. Damn the traditions of this frozen land. Her husband should be by her side as their child entered the world.

As if in response to her unspoken plea, King Ozias sprinted back to the royal birthing chambers, bursting open the doors.

"We all need to get out of here as quickly as we can. Everyone needs to get to caverns," ordered Ozias. He blinked fast as though processing information. Quick breaths filled his chest.

"What is going on?" Lyshyla asked.

"Iceoth is under invasion; colonial forces have arrived on our shores," Ozias said.

"Yes, Onissa's attack made that clear," Lyshyla said, wiping at Oadira's forehead. "We should have at least another day until even the first scouts arrive, though."

Ozias grabbed several blankets from the bed across the room. "Onissa's sneak attack may have failed, but she had a larger force with her. Our Anubis guards defeated them, but another battalion was hidden in the snow drifts outside the city. They started attacking the refugees and are making their way into the city. We must go now."

"The queen is only one to two centimeters dilated," Lyshyla said as she grabbed Ozia's arm to slow him down. "If we leave now, we can get to the caverns to save the children. I'll have the midwives started praying over Queen Oadira, asking Ibeji to extend her labor until she is safe to deliver them."

"Did you say 'children'?" Ozias asked.

"Yes, triplets," the lead midwife said, stepping forward. Long dreadlocks were tied up on top of her head in a towering bouffant. "During the queen's pregnancy I saw signs, but only now that labor has commence can we confirm. You and the queen will have not one, but three children this day."

"By the blessings of Ibeji," King Ozias said. He grabbed Oadira's hand and squeezed it against the Marula pole.

Triplets. How was this possible?

She knew how it was possible, of course, but the thought of having three children inside her womb made Oadira sweat even more. Being mother to one baby would be hard enough, but three? Were even a king and queen equipped for such a challenge?

Ozias seemed to grow lightheaded and sat down in the chair near the door. Just then, his stepfather, Steward Nilhist, and Ozia's best friend and servant Ossa, entered the room at a run.

"We have to get out of the city and to the caverns now," Nilhist stressed through lumbered breaths. "I've given the evacuation order, but we've all been taken by surprise. I knew Onissa had infiltrated the city with her personal guard, but I had no idea she commanded forces that had secretly made it so close to Benin."

"We must hurry," Ozias said, standing back up. "How close are the colonial forces that landed yesterday?"

"Mere hours away from the city," Ossa replied as he wiped sweat from his brow.

"Let's go!" Ozia ordered, waving his hand toward the door. "Grab the thick traveling cloaks. The snow isn't as deep as it was a few weeks ago, but outside the city it is still cold enough to freeze everyone. Be prepared!"

Midwives rushed to Oadira's side, helping her to stand. The contractions seemed to have subsided somewhat, allowing Oadira to breathe a bit easier.

"Where are we going?" she asked.

"To the caverns of refuge," Ozias said as he took her hand.

The group ran down the hall toward the stairs leading to the banquet hall and court chambers. Just as they reached the landing overlooking the entry hall below, a contraction hit Oadira, and she was forced to stop. The world spun around her. This was not the circumstances she imagined for the birth of her child…children.

"Give her a moment," Lyshyla said.

"While we're here," Steward Nilhist said, placing his hand on Ozia's shoulder. "I need to tell you some things quickly just in case we're all separated. I'm fully aware of Nygaard's prophecy, mentioning the Black Madonna would fall in love with an heir descended from Kemettian bloodline. The Madonna would assume authority as queen, her lover as king, superseding my right over the Ancient Bloodline. Those were the terms that allowed Nygaard to leave Sahael with his people as an independent bloodline. They all traveled through the Nabtahenge Gates from Sahael to get to Iceoth."

"Was this when Sahael was infiltrated and destroyed?" Ozias asked.

"No, in Nygaard's Nalace journal he said that he observed a man in Necrosis's Chamber who had been there for some time. He said that the man was dressed in a black cloak and all black garb. He tried using the Nabtahenge Gates but was unable to open them. He overheard the man talking about moving coffins to undisclosed locations."

"Did the man know Nygaard was present?" Ozias asked.

"No. Nygaard followed the man and watched as he dug up Nzingha's obsidian key from the center of where the dead rested. According to Nygaard's Nalace journal, the man in black took the key, killing the Medjay Gate guardians and gate navigators, preventing the gates from ever being active again."

"Why do we need to know this?" Oadira asked as her contraction subsided.

"I know you've been searching for the gates on Iceoth," Nilhist said. "I don't know where they are, and the journal didn't say, but Nygaard wrote that after Nzingha's obsidian key was in his possession, the man in black rubbed his obsidian ring and opened up a portal that he entered and was not seen again. There may be another way to travel to Sahael that doesn't require the gates. A report reached my ears a few days ago about someone seeing a man in a black cloak leading a small Ennead force on the shores of Iceoth. Now that winter has ended, I thought we could research together, but if we're forced to flee now, you should know this information."

"Who was the man in black?" Ozias asked.

Nilhist glanced at Oadira as she stood back up, ready to continue their flight. "Nygaard said that the man in black's name was Damien. He was following the orders of his father, Natas, who wanted all the Ancient Bloodlines destroyed. He wore a cloak so dark no light could escape it. He could blend into shadow and remain unseen."

Natas. Could Oadira ever escape that name? His anger seemed eternal, never resting, always seeking her and her cousins. Was he on the shores of Iceoth right now, commanding his forces to march through the snow, not caring how many of them dies along the way so long as he achieved his ultimate purpose?

"What happened to Nygaard's Nalace journal?" Ozias asked as they started down the flight of stairs again. "Oadira and I never found anything like that in the archives."

"It was given to the sirens by Lyshyla the day you arrived in Iceoth," Nilhist answered. "I'm sorry. I feared the Signs of the Times. I was a coward."

"Thank you, Father," Ozias said. "We'll deal with all of this later."

They made their way to the palace entrance, past the ice throne, and down the stairs. By the time they reached the throne room, Ozias carried Oadira so she wouldn't have to run. Outside the palace, cold air hit Oadira's cheeks. She wanted to return to the warmth and comfort of the birthing suite. Shouts filled her ears though, and she realized no one would be comfortable this day. Citizens of Benin ran in all directions, children holding the hands of their parents, carrying whatever supplies would fit on their backs. The city was being evacuated.

"To the stables!" Ossa said. He pointed toward a stone building to their left with tall archways and trees with the first buds of the spring thaw.

They stepped into the stables and Oadira saw their transportation would consist of kelpies; shape-changing, aquatic, cream-colored horses that lived by the water. They were powerful, blue-eyed beasts, loyal to the Orishan bloodline. Oadira had only seen them a handful of times, since they were only used by the royal family, and even then, only in times of great need. Kelpies were sacred, and thus treated like royalty themselves.

"Can you ride, my queen?" Lyshyla asked.

"I can," Oadira grimaced as Ozias put her down. "Trust in my strength, and I'll trust in yours."

"If we leave now when the colonial forces arrive, no one will be here," alerted Ossa.

"We'll use the carriage," Ozias said. "I won't have my wife riding as she's giving birth. Ossa, you'll drive the team. Anubis guard, you're with me."

King Ozias gently placed Queen Oadira in the carriage sled pulled by two kelpies with Ossa at the reins. He sat beside her in the sled as they made their way to the outside of Benin City. "Let's get to the clearing as quickly as we can. Once we get there, we can lose them in Wahangara Forest."

The kelpies rode them all toward the east, away from the coast. After a half hour they split into two groups to confuse the colonial forces.

"The majority of my private guard will travel with me, and the other half will travel with Lyshyla to the caverns," the king declared.

"The queen should travel with me," said Lyshyla.

"No! My wife will travel with me," Ozias demanded with authority.

"Apologies, my king. I will travel with the second group," Lyshyla said.

"My father will travel with you as well," Ozias ordered.

They split up, heading in separate directions. King Ozias and Queen Oadira continued traveling east, while Lyshyla and the king's men headed southwest.

The colonial cavalry pursued Ozias and Oadira around the bend and down each icy path, until Ossa managed to lose them for a short time among a herd of orange haired mammoths. Oadira had never seen such beasts before, with their long snouts and shaggy hair. Had their situation not been so dire, she would have stopped and spent time with the creatures, but such detours were a luxury they could not afford. They entered a clearing, with a forest of evergreen trees covered in snow on their right. Ossa stopped the wagon and went out to speak with the king and queen.

"We lost them for now," Ossa said. "We need to create a diversion and make them think we've headed in a different direction. I'll send one of the kelpies in one direction and have a group of our soldiers continue straight toward the plains, forcing the colonials to divide their forces. I will then take the carriage sled in another direction, allowing you and the queen time to escape into the forest on foot. Make a shelter and I will come back and find you once we've lost the colonials. Use the ice cornices toward the forest so no footprints will be evident in the snow until you reach the tree line."

King Ozias agreed. He took Ossa's hand into his and nodded his head. Ossa ordered a small cohort of troops to remain as they headed in three different directions.

Ozias and Oadira made their way into an icy clearing with a handful of soldiers. Again, Ozias carried his wife. Oadira loved him more in that moment than she ever had before. Contractions continued sporadically and without warning. Tiny snow crystals fell from the sky. King Ozias peered around the area, searching for shelter as he carried his pregnant queen.

"I need to stop and rest for a moment," he said, his breath turning frosty in the air. "The ice in the drifts is too slick to carry you, my dear. I can barely keep my balance. You'll have to walk on foot for a time."

Queen Oadira nodded her head in agreement. "You have done more than any husband should have to. I am strong. Pregnant with three babies apparently, but strong."

Ozias chuckled and brushed snowflakes from his forehead. "Triplets. Today has not been the day I expected it to be. Let us move to the trees."

They made their way into the forest, using the using the frozen edges of the snowdrifts so as not to leave behind evidence of their flight. Silence reigned between the trees as if no sound could enter the woodland.

Oadira took a few steps before seeing a spot of red on the snow next to a tree. It appeared to be blood.

"Look!" Oadira said.

"What is it?" Ozias asked. Before Oadira could answer, Ozias gasped in complete shock. It wasn't just blood on the snow.

The corpses of dead colonials lay all around beneath the trees. They looked fresh, limbs torn from their bodies and stomachs ripped open as if gnawed on by some wild animal.

"What happened here?" Queen Oadira breathed. She hadn't seen anything like this before, not even on the night of the rebellion at the Lalaurie plantation.

"Frost apes are lurking in the forest," a guard whispered. Holding his sword in the direction of the bodies. "They've just finished feeding and will be back. Look at the impressions in the snow."

While trampled, the dirty snow showed evidence of large footprints in the shape of thick hands, complete with opposable thumbs.

"What are frost apes?" Queen Oadira asked.

Ozias swallowed. "Keep walking…slowly."

The group shifted to the left and began walking around the dead bodies. No sound beyond their feet crunching in the snow disturbed their progress.

"Frost apes," Ozias began, barely above a whisper, "are large, hairy, fifteen-foot beasts with thick, white coats of fur. They have bluish-red eyes, and yellow fangs for teeth. They hide in the snow, stalking their prey before surprising them with a blindside attack, killing them instantly. The frost apes dined on their flesh, ripping them to pieces. Obviously, a battalion of colonials tried to make it through the forest. Their misfortune is our gain. This will give us the time we need to find somewhere safe. Let's just leave them alone and let these frost apes continue to feed upon the dead soldiers when they come back."

"Are you sure?" Oadira asked, eyes focused on the severed head of a soldier at her feet.

"Yes," Ozias answered. "The apes seem to have fed not long ago and shouldn't be back for more until a bit later. They are consistent creatures."

The group moved quietly through the woods, entering a grove of snow-covered Marula Trees unlike anything Oadira had ever seen before. Their leaves were still green, but a layer of frost covered every limb as if the tree rested dormant in the white environment.

Oadira slowed. Her contractions grew more intense as numbness entered her legs.

"Let's hurry. If we don't pick up our pace, the frost apes will catch up to us and find another meal," Ozias urged.

"My strength is waning," Oadira said. She felt disappointment at her fatigue, but realized she was in labor and had been for hours now. Her children would be arriving soon, and her body knew it.

"I understand, my love. Will you be, okay?" Ozias asked.

"The lives within me are draining me of all my energy," Oadira said weakly just before she tumbled to the ground. Ozias jumped quickly and helped his wife to her feet. "I am sorry, my love, I am slowing us down. I will try to move faster."

"You are too weak to travel." Ozias waved over his personal guard. "You will not make it to the caverns in your current condition. It's best if you rest here for a while. I will construct an igloo to keep you safe and warm until I can find a way to get us to the caverns. Guards! Start forming bricks of ice and snow so our queen can be out of the elements. We'll need any extra blankets or cloaks we have so she can be warm and comfortable. After that, I want a pair of you to search for a path to the caverns."

Within moments it seemed to Oadira's tired mind, the igloo was completed. Ozias moved his wife inside as the Anubis guard stood watch with their swords and shields. Snow began to fall again.

"Alert us of any disturbance," Ozias ordered as he followed Oadira inside. The igloo was small but comfortable, with blankets piled all around for Oadira to sit on and wrap herself. The air was already warmer and more pleasant than outside in the forest. "The constant snowfall will keep us hidden from the frost apes, snow sabers, and lynxes," Ozias continued.

Using her Orishan abilities, Oadira manifested a warm cerulean shield around her body. Her shivering stopped and her body warmed.

King Ozias took his queen's hand. "The colonial forces will hunt us down until they catch and enslave us. It's their way of life now."

"Eventually, we're going to have to find a way off this island," Oadira said.

"First, we should concentrate on removing the colonials from Iceoth. I refuse to allow our land or our people to ever come under colonial control," Ozias spat.

Oadira rested, but after several hours one of the guards called to Ozias. After speaking with the guard outside, Ozias returned.

"We need to go," he said. "The forest is no longer quiet. Apes howl to the south, and the guards have seen wolves running through the trees. It's getting to late afternoon as well. The forest will only get more dangerous as night falls. We're no longer safe here."

"I don't know how far I can go," Oadira breathed. The thought of stepping out into the cold and walking for miles while contractions continued to plague her randomly made her want to lie down and never get up again.

"We'll find you transport," Ozias said, helping his wife to stand. "I promise."

The group continued moving through the forest, passing evergreen trees accented by the occasional Marula. After less than a half hour, Oadira cried out as a powerful contraction almost knocked her onto her back. The cry echoed through the forest, answered by a wolf's howl. Within moments a wild pack of dire wolves darted through the trees and growled at the soldiers and royal couple.

"Stay behind us!" a guard shouted.

More wolves made their way through the trees. Oadira counted twenty-four, double the number of people in their small group. The wolves growled and snuck forward before running back to the pack as if testing the guards' resolve. Could each of the Anubis soldiers take out two wolves, while Oadira and Ozias took out two of their own?

Doubtful.

As if aware of their advantage, the wolves swarmed forward.

"Protect the Queen!" one of the soldiers yelled, swinging his sword at an advancing dire wolf.

"I'll die protecting you!" Ozias cried. A luminous, blue light emitted from Njiru's ring on King Ozias's finger, triggering the illumination of his eyes and tattoos. The light spread with an aura that covered his entire body in sapphire. The cobalt aura transformed into an indestructible Sahaelian shield, protecting him from head to toe.

Oadira smiled. She and her husband were one. Her powers were his. She no longer feared the beasts of the forest.

The dire wolves were quick, fast, and ferocious. One of them lunged forward. King Ozias used his Orishan artes to conjure a heavy shield that the dire wolf rammed into repelling it back. Another dire wolf attacked King Ozias from behind. He turned the shield and conjured up a Lunette spear, thrusting it into the forehead of the dire wolf, killing it instantly.

Blood splattered the snow as wolves fell before the Anubis guard and King Ozias' assault. Even so, several soldiers fell, screaming in pain as wolves slashed their flesh.

Ozias fought, using two conjured blades of Orichalcum to stab, puncture, and slice off the heads of the attacking dire wolves. Oadira closed her eyes and breathed, giving what strength she had to her husband to protect their unborn children. After a few more minutes, Ozias breathed heavily, drenched in dire wolf blood. The few dire wolves that remained stopped and peered across the blood-stained snow and exposed entrails of their fallen brethren. They ran off, leaving the group of humans to regroup.

"Your highness," a soldier said, grabbing Oadira by the arms as she swayed back and forth.

"We're okay!" another called.

"Quashrum has fallen!" another cried. "And Kutaba."

"Leave them!" Ozias ordered, voice thundering through the wood. "We don't have time for anything else. Any apes in the area will have heard the fight. We need to move now." He pointed at two of the guards next to him. "You men! Carry your queen. I will lead the way."

The guards hoisted Oadira between them while two other soldiers supported her weight as well. Ozias walked in front of the group, tattoos glowing on his exposed neck, while his conjured blades still dripped wolf's blood. Several soldiers whispered in awe about the king's abilities and prowess in the fight.

They wandered as best they could in the direction of the caverns, but the forest appeared to be a labyrinth. They came upon a frozen river as the sun began to set. Oadira longed for the day to end. She had no idea how close the birth was at this point, but her contractions would come and go, leaving her for an hour at a time before roaring back more powerful than before.

As dusk began to darken the forest, one of the Anubis guards ran up to Ozias. “My king,” he said. “One of our advanced scouts you sent to find a way through the forests has tracked us and made his way back. He hasn’t found any paths but has alerted us to a military unit making their way in our direction right now. They aren’t colonials…but are marked with the armor of the Ennead, bearing the Ankh symbol.”

“Hide, now!” Ozias ordered. The guards holding Oadira raced to a grove of Marula trees and crouched in a crook next to the king. After a few minutes, Oadira could hear the crunching of the snow beneath the feet of numerous people not far away from them.

“Look!” a soldier to Oadira’s left whispered. “The Ennead.”

A line of hundreds of soldiers consisting of warriors covered in black, metallic armor with gray robes draping their bodies, all standing seven feet tall, trudged through the clearing just beyond the trees. Many of them held the ends of canvas stretchers with what Oadira thought at first were wounded combatants, but in the fading light, soon realized were the dead bodies they had seen of the colonial forces attacked by the apes. After another minute, several soldiers passed carrying the remains of the two fallen Anubis warriors they had been forced to leave to the wolves less than an hour before.

“What are they doing with the bodies?” Oadira asked. “Why carry them out, especially when they don’t belong to their army?”

“The Ennead are responsible for the departed hearing the dead sing Nova’s song,” the guard to her left breathed. “They’re retrieving bodies due to the increasing death toll mounting in Iceoth. They are here to take the bodies back to Naharis's realm in the south."

"But why?"

Before the guard could answer, the last of the Ennead passed, followed closely by a man in a black cloak and all black garb, face covered.

"By the gods," Ozias whispered. "The man in the black cloak."

"Is that the man your father spoke of?" Oadira asked. "The one from the journal? Could it really be Nata's son?"

The legion passed and the sounds of their footsteps grew fainter. Darkness fell in the forest and the temperatures dropped even further.

Ozias took a deep breath. "It's now or never. Safety is our main concern. We need to find shelter for the night. Perhaps we can build another igloo for the queen."

"No," Oadira said as a contraction threatened to send her falling to the snow. "The men will freeze out here. We have to keep moving…I can't have…anyone else dying for…"

"Sir!" a guard said, grabbing Ozias' shoulder. "We're hearing ape calls from the south. The queen is right. We can't stay here. Plus, if the Ennead decide to come back, we can't possibly defeat them. Movement is our only option."

"My wife can't make it another step!" Ozias shouted. "We've pushed her the entire day while she's been in labor. She'll freeze to death if we don't make a shelter. She doesn't have strength---"

Oadira touched Ozias' hand. "I have strength…enough," she grimaced as pain washed over her body. "Give…me some of…your strength, my love. I will find us…a path."

A warmth spread through Oadira's body as she pulled strength from her husband's body. The blades he held in his hand dissolved in the cold darkness. Oadira closed her eyes, feeling the minds of the creatures around her.

"I can feel the emotions of the animals," Oadira said weakly. "I can feel the paths."

She heard the sounds and sights of the forest as only an inhabitant could. The trees felt giant. The stones felt like mountains. The lakes felt like oceans, and the birds were just as dangerous as the sabers and lynxes.

She knew where to go.

"The path in the center," Oadira pointed.

"Carry her!" Ozias ordered his men.

They traveled down the path, bombarded by sweeping winds ready to cast them into the cavernous trenches where spikes protruded from the darkness. Ozias trudged forward, his arm in front of his face as a shield. All warmth seemed to leave Oadira to the point where she felt like she would never feel warm ever again.

"Where do we go next?" Ozias asked. "It's too dark. I can't see anything."

"I'm too weak to use my abilities," Oadira admitted, slumping into her escort's shoulders.

"What can I do to help?" Ozias asked, voice cracking with emotion.

Seek the guidance of the higher powers, Oadira answered telepathically.

King Ozias fell to his knees. *I don't know what to do. How can I know what to do at this moment right now? The men are freezing. You're freezing!*

Search within yourself for answers, Oadira replied. *We were meant to be together. Solomon told me the gods were on my side in saving our people. They won't leave us to die. Not here; not tonight. Our children will be a force for good. The gods won't turn their face from us. I don't believe they will.*

Minds linked, Oadira saw the image of a whistle in her husband's thoughts.

"The whistle," Ozias said slowly. He reached into his pocket and pulled out the lover's whistle his father had given him after Onissa's attack that morning. "The sirens."

"Sirens are not…forgiving creatures," Oadira groaned as another contraction hit her stomach. "Your father already called them today…"

"I don't care," Ozias said, putting the whistle to his lips. "Whatever sacrifice they require, I'll accept."

He blew into it, imitating the distress call of a siren Nilhist had used that morning. Within seconds, several sirens descended upon their location through the snow overhead.

"You have summoned us, my young king. What is it you need?" Ujana asked.

"My wife requires assistance. Help us please, grandmother," King Ozias said.

Oadira smiled as she fought through the pain of her labor.

"Can you transport us to the caverns?" Ozias pleaded. "We're freezing to death. My wife, the queen, has been in labor all day. Please, show us mercy!"

"It is not our duty to show mercy," Ujana said, voice emotionless. Her wings flapped, casting off the snow accumulating on her feathers. "We have already served you this day at the request of the one my daughter loved. You may be my stepson, but our place is not to serve the lower beings needlessly."

"She is a Black Madona!" Ozias screamed. "She carries the future of Sahael in her womb. Save her and our children! Leave the rest of us." He held out the whistle in his palm. "Take the whistle so I can never use it again if you must! Just please…save my wife."

Ujana glanced at the whistle and then to Oadira. "You may keep the whistle for now, king of Benin. And we will take your queen to the caverns so her children may be born."

"What about…" Oadira said, trying to stand but finding blackness creeping around her field of vision.

"Take her," Ujana said, pointing at Oadira. "Leave the others."

"No!" Oadira screamed. "Don't leave him! Don't leave him to freeze!"

Strong hands grasped Oadira and lifted her up as she reached for Ozias. Her husband looked at her as the sirens pulled Oadira toward the cold sky. Ozias grew smaller in her eyes but mountainous in her heart. She screamed, but her own voice grew distant in her ears.

Ozias! Ozias!

You're safe, my love. You will be safe.

Not without you!

Nothing will keep me from you. Nothing! Trust in that.

Blackness enveloped Oadira and she faded from consciousness.

CHAPTER II

THE WAR FOR ICEOTH

Iceoth, Wahangara Forest, Snow Caverns

Oadira awoke in a room of stone with polished ceilings and a fireplace carved into the wall. Before she had a moment to think about sirens or wolves or Ozias freezing to death, a contraction hit her so hard she screamed.

The babies were coming. Now.

Midwives surrounded her, along with Lyshyla, and her closest female servants. Thery took Oadira and had her squat on the ground in the center of the birthing chamber.

"What do I do?" Oadira grimaced.

"I'll help you get through this process," Lyshyla said, holding her from behind by Oadira's armpits. "The first thing you need to do is grab the Marula pole to help steady your body."

Oadira grabbed the wooden pole.

"Aw! My legs are numb, and I can barely stand," Oadira said.

"It's all right. I'll help you stand, then you need to push as hard as you can if you want to remove the numbness from your legs."

Oadira pushed and moaned as contractions came in wave after wave.

"You're doing it! You're doing it! Keep pushing!" Lyshyla said.

The contraction intensified and then released. Something landed softly on the pillow a few inches below Oadira's crouched form. Oadira wanted a better look at her child, but the contractions didn't stop.

"Okay—that's one—just two more left," Lyshyla said.

"Are you serious? That was just one?" Oadira yelled.

"Yes, you have to keep pushing," Lyshyla said.

"Okay, hmph!"

"That's it! That's it! Push!" Lyshyla said.

The second child dropped on the soft feather ground.

"There's one more left. C'mon, you have to push," Lyshyla said.

Oadira took a deep breath. "I can't. I'm too tired. I can't do this anymore. My body is tired," Oadira said, holding onto the pole with her hands.

"You must keep pushing. If you want to rest, you must deliver your third child," Lyshyla said. "Only then can the midwives care for them and wash their bodies."

"I'm so lightheaded," Queen Oadira said, who began to fade in and out of consciousness. "Where's Ozias? Has he arrived from the forest? Where's my husband?"

"Stay with me. You're almost done. You must keep pushing if you want to save your third child's life," Lyshyla said.

Oadira pushed as hard as she could, giving birth to the third baby. Instantly all pressure ceased, and a wave of calm washed over her.

"You've done it!" Lyshyla shouted. "Congratulations, now you must cut the umbilical cords with your mouth, as is the royal custom."

Oadira had been waiting for this from the moment she realized she was pregnant. While an unpleasant thought, the severing of the umbilical cord was the true separation of mother from child and seen as the first great sacrifice of motherhood. Oadira did it willingly, biting off the umbilical cords to each of her children and pushed out her placenta, urinating on it to ensure she'd be fertile once more. After that, the midwives took the children to a wash basin on the other side of the room and Lyshyla helped Oadira to her bed to rest. Faint cries began to fill the chamber as the children breathed on their own for the first time.

"Congratulations my queen," one of the midwives said with a bow. "You have given birth to three strong sons. They will be a blessing to the world and the people of Benin. May Ibeji bless their lives and your fertility until the sun rises no more."

Oadira's midwives held the three newborns for her to look at. Three strong, Black, healthy baby boys with striking dark blue eyes. Overcome with emotion, sapphire tears streamed down Oadira's cheeks. Lyshyla rubbed her forehead and smiled broadly.

The midwives handed the first baby to Oadira, and she took him into her left arm. They gave her the second and third as well, allowing the children to bond with their mother. All four sets of their cerulean eyes shone brightly.

Eventually the babies were placed in small, wooden bassinets right next to Oadira.

Oadira wanted to sleep, but now that the births were

completed, energy rushed through her veins.

"Where is Ozias?" she asked.

Lyshyla nodded and left the room, returning moments later with Nilhist. The former king had a look of both pride and worry as he glanced at his grandchildren resting in their bassinets. Sapphire tears ran down his cheeks, running down his white beard. Nilhist reached down and held each boy one at a time and blessed them with a special prayer. After blessing the babies, he placed one of them back into Oadira's arms, another into the arms of one of the second midwives, and the last child into the arms of the first midwife.

"The sirens brought you to us safely," Nilhist said. "I honored them, but they are…difficult to please at times. I am grateful for their kindness even so."

"Where is Ozias and the Anubis Guards?" Oadira questioned. She had seen them fade into the white of the forest as the sirens pulled her into the cold night.

Nilhist glanced at the floor. "I don't know. The colonial forces hit with far more speed and potency than I imagined possible. It was as if the wings of demons were pushing them onward."

"Natas," Oadira whispered. If Natas had indeed ordered the strike, his lieutenants would have stopped at nothing, forcing their troops to the point of death to achieve even the smallest victory.

"Yes, Natas," Nilhist confirmed. "I know you're tired, Oadira, and you're worried about Ozias, but you are the queen of this people now. You must know what I know, and act to the best of your ability. I just received word the colonial forces are invading the cities of Nioni, Erie, Kuma, and Okap."

"What about the city of Ogden?" Lyshyla asked.

"The forces destroyed the city," informed Nilhist. "Only a

single survivor lives to tell the tale."

"What else can you tell me?" Oadira asked.

"Benin City is gone, your majesty," said Nilhist in a grave tone. "The colonial general Vipsanius obliterated it. Entries and exits have been closed off. The Orishan people must travel through the caverns to be safe."

So that was it. In a single day, the city of Benin was destroyed and the people of Iceoth scattered or enslaved.

Just like Sahael.

Oadira wanted to scream and thrash and break every piece of furniture in the cavernous room, but Nilhist was right. She was queen.

"Do you have suggestions, Steward of Benin?" Oadira asked.

"Someone has to go back out there and save the people," Nilhist replied.

"I agree," said Oadira. She stood, wrapping herself in a robe lying next to her bed. While her legs ached from the previous day's journey, and fatigue pulled at her sore muscles, the warmth of anger seemed to strengthen her.

Lyshyla folded her arms, a look of determination on her face. "A lot of our people will be fleeing toward the caverns and the sacred pyramid, which will expose our location. Ossa made it here last night after splitting up your group. He informed us of a line of refugees trying to find the paths that lead here. If the colonial army discovers their flight, we will be trapped in these caves."

"Something has to be done about that," Oadira said. She scratched her chin, thinking about all the books and histories she had read while studying with Ozias in the archives. "How about using the city guards who can enter the cities safely to direct the people to the clearing beyond Arrion Mountain? If colonial forces should follow, they can be taken out by ambush."

"Dispatch the scouts to ensure the terrain is safe and clear for the rest of us," Nilhist nodded. "Good strategy. This plan is all well and good, but don't forget, we need to speak with the council to determine the best course of action. Not all the regents made it, but enough for a quorum. We must respect tradition and share our thoughts with the leading families."

"I wish to meet with the council," said Oadira. "I have regained most of my strength. Allow me to dress and join you all in the war council chamber with the babies."

"You should rest," Lyshyla said, stepping toward Oadira.

"I am queen, and now," Oadira informed with a raised hand. "I can sleep later. For now, our people suffer. We need to meet this crisis head-on…and we need to find Ozias."

Lass than an hour later Oadira sat at the head of a large stone table in a dark cavern room lit by torches. Three basinets sat against the wall, each with a midwife tending to the three newborn boys. Despite the joy of the royal birth, the regents had no time for children or familial emotion. The council members, all men, gathered around Oadira and Nilhist, arguing about how to best deal with the intruding colonial forces.

"How can we help the people of Iceoth get here safely?" a council member with long dreadlock and a green robe asked.

"There needs to be a plan," a second council member

shouted as he scratched his greying beard.

"How can it be executed to get them all here safely?" a third council member asked.

Male voices roared as they debated the best way to overcome the challenges facing the people and Iceoth.

"The people have been evacuated from the cities and are making their way toward the clearing," Nilhist announced, hands in the air to silence the argument. He placed a map in front of him and Oadira and pointed at a valley between two mountain ranges. "Queen Oadira came up with a plan, and less than an hour ago I sent word for our troops to follow her council. Our spies are in the refugee groups and assisted them by helping those from the destroyed cities get to the clearing here between mount Arrion and the Nagritan range. We are setting up a trap for the incoming colonial forces to end the war and to prevent them from coming to Iceoth again."

"All the people in the neighboring cities are going to be safe," Oadira said.

"Allow me to search for King Ozias and the Anubis guard," Lyshyla said.

"Queen Oadira needs you here," Nilhist said.

Oadira shook her head. "I have more than enough help. Dispatch Lyshyla to the forest and any able men who can carry a sword should be armed and sent to the clearing. We're using the refugees as bait, and we won't leave them to die."

The council members grumbled a bit for a moment, but seemed to agree with Oadira's leadership, however grudgingly.

"Then mobilize the army and split them into two groups," Nilhist said, thumping his hand against the map. "One group will travel to Nioni, Kuma, and Erie to help the remaining stragglers and come upon the colonial army's rear. The second army is to head to Okap, Benin, and Ogden to gather the weak and then meet them in the clear opening of Iceoth. Once the colonial army is in the clear, both armies will converge on General Vipsanius's colonial army and wipe them out for good."

As the council ended their gathering and made their way from the war chamber, Oadira grabbed Lyshyla by the arm.

"When we were in the forest," Oadira began. The memory of the man in black and his silent army stuck in her mind, particularly with Ozias missing. She had no desire for her husband, dead or alive, to be found by such a force. "We came upon an Ennead legion. They were led by a man in a black cloak that blended in with the shadows themselves as if light was trapped in its folds, similar to what Steward Nilhist mentioned before we left Benin. The soldiers appeared to be gathering dead bodies. Not just their own, but those of witans from the colonial army and even some of our dead Anubis Guard. Why are they doing this? Have you read anything about this practice?"

"It's recently been their practice," Lyshyla said.

Nilhist shook hands with a departing regent and stepped over to the women. "You saw the man in the black cloak?"

"When we were in Wahangara Forest," she nodded. "They were collecting the dead."

Rubbing his forehead, Nilhist let out a nervous breath. "The Demir are responsible for retrieving the dead, and if they are responsible for retrieving the dead, we will continue to let them do their job. Unless you think we should investigate it further, my queen."

"It matters not; we need to figure out how we can save the people first," Oadira said. Even as the words left her lips though, an uneasy feeling crept up her spine. Perhaps it was the Demir simply clearing potential battlefields of bodies…or perhaps it was something more sinister. Oadira trusted her instincts now enough to know there was more going on here than she or Nilhist wished.

"What do you suggest, Queen Oadira?" Lyshyla asked.

Glancing at the bassinets as two of her sons began crying, Oadira came to a conclusion.

"Let me breastfeed my sons and eat some food myself. After that, I go with you, Father-in-Law, to help our people. I will lead one army, you the other."

"No," Lyshyla said, shaking her head. "You are in no state to---"

"I am in every state to help my people," Oadira said firmly. "My sons will be taken care of by the midwives. They will be fine for the next few days. If we don't stop this invasion, these caverns won't be safe for them anyway. There will be nowhere safe on this entire continent."

"You have never been in battle," Nilhist replied.

"My entire life was a battle!" Oadira shouted. "I saw the plantation slaves raped and murdered while was unable to do anything to help them because I was afraid. I saw children branded and broken. I saw every horror you can imagine. Don't tell me I've never seen battle. I've seen things your son has never witnessed from within the walls of your palace. I will lead an army and I will help save this people and I will revenge myself of those who would enslave me!"

Silence fell. Both Lyshyla and Nilhist lowered their heads.

With reluctant pause, Lyshyla agreed. "I will send Ossa with you as your personal protection."

"Ossa will want to go with you to find Ozias in the forest," Oadira protested. "Ossa is his best friend."

Nilhist put his hand on Oadira's shoulder. "Yes, and if

Ozias were here, he would want Ossa by your side to keep you safe, not searching for him."

Now it was Oadira's turn to reluctantly nod in agreement.

Preparations had already been made, and after only a few hours, former King Nilhist took half the army to travel from city to city until he reached the clearing, with the second army, led by Oadira and Ossa, traveling to Benin to search for remaining refugees.

Making her way down the northeastern coast that afternoon, Ozias entered the city of Benin. The city lay in ruins, smoke rising from burned homes and the torched palace that the day before had served as Oadira's home. Death and destruction everywhere. Lifeless bodies of men, women, and children lay bloodied with exposed flesh and soulless pupils staring into an endless winter. While making their way up the ridgeline outside the city, Oadira and her men encountered another sizable group of Ennead soldiers in the valley below them, more than a mile away.

"I've never seen them in such large numbers," Ossa said, pointing at a line of dark-skinned warriors in their elaborate gray armor. Red flags emblazoned with the Narsan symbol of Natas waved in the cold breeze; the square symbol of the four L's symbolizing Narsa. Many of the soldiers carried briers with three or four dead bodies piled on top of each other. "They outnumber us two to one."

"What are they doing?" Oadira asked, noticing again the penchant for collecting the dead.

"It seems they are going out of their way to round up every dead body that has had the breath of life leave it," Ossa said.

The Ennead continued piling up dead bodies, as the Nethanite Body Retrievers loaded them onto wagons. As Oadira and her army watched, the enemy force turned away from their position at the top of the ridge and began marching toward the coast.

"They seem to have no care about the war at all," Oadira breathed. "They don't appear to have fought any battles. Even from here you can see how shiny their armor is. What are they doing?"

By late afternoon the temperatures had warmed slightly and Oadira's force made it to their position on the south side of the clearing.

General Vipsanius and his colonial army had already made their way into the clearing to attack the refugees that had gathered there.

Exactly as Oadira had hoped.

A horn blew as General Vipsanius ordered his forces to attack the vulnerable inhabitants running from his army. The refugees coalesced in the valley center, completely exposing the witan general's whole army to the hidden forces.

Another horn blew, this one from across the clearing. Nilhist's legions rushed from the trees of Wahangara Forest and descended into the valley, much to the surprise of the invading force.

"Attack!" Oadira cried. Her own army sprinted forward over the ridgeline and advanced on the general's men. The archers fired on the colonial forces at a moment's notice on the command of Ossa. The soldiers were prepared on both sides of the clearing, attacking the colonial army with the goal of wiping them out entirely.

"Archers attack now! We need to provide cover for the refugees," Ossa ordered.

"First flank, attack!" Oadira ordered as Nilhist's men continued attacking from the right side of Wahangara Forest.

The armies crashed into each other like two waves, filling the valley with the shouts and cries of battle. Oadira shouted commands and her men followed her every direction. As one section of the colonial army attempted to break through their lines, Oadira moved more men to bottle them in. The white snow soon turned red all around. Taking pains to make sure the refugees they'd used as bait were protected, Oadira pushed her military hard in the opposite direction, absolutely crushing her enemy between her men and those of Steward Nilhist.

"Second flank, attack!" Oadira ordered as she faced General Vipsanius's army head on. She followed behind the leading legion, stepping over witan bodies as they advanced. Ossa remained by her side, ever ready to defend her should a stray soldier make it through the lines.

"Third flank, attack," former King Nilhist ordered from a nearby snowbank, now close enough to Oadira to shout her name. "We have General Vipsanius trapped on three sides," he waved his sword. "He is looking to take the path of least resistance."

"I'll order the last section of the army to attack them from the rear, boxing him in and forcing him to fight on all sides," Oadira cried back.

"We are going to be fighting into the night under a blood moon as red iron fills the air," Ossa said, looking up into the skies. "Are you alright, my queen?"

Oadira didn't know how to answer. She had only slept a few hours over the past two days. She had given birth to triplets. She had fled from her home and then seen it destroyed.

She should be exhausted.

She should be unable to walk or think or feel.

And yet, energy like she had never felt before coursed through her veins. She could fight for hours, days, if it meant destroying these men who had tried to enslave her people. She could fight a thousand battles and not break a sweat. It had been some time since she had allowed herself to feel the emotions of the people around her, but now she seemed to feed on their apprehension, swallowing their bloodlust, and soaking up their nervous energy, making it her own.

Night fell and the battle continued unabated. Thousands fell by the sword, and still Oadira pushed her soldiers forward. She had lost sight of Nilhist hours before, and hoped her father-in-law survived the night.

At the beginning of the third watch, Ossa returned from having met with a few of their generals in the field. He carried a torch and looked more exhausted than Oadira had ever seen him.

"General Vipsanius's colonial militia has suffered a significant blow," he said. "He's lost twenty thousand infantrymen leaving twenty thousand in the open, exposed to the firing arrows coming down at them. That should kill another eight thousand of his colonial forces within the hour. We're running low on arrows, but we dispatched a group to gather more form the battlefield."

"What of Nilhist?" she asked.

"I don't know, my queen. I've been hearing rumors that he faced First Ennead Commander Shu in single combat, but I cannot confirm whether that's true or not. In any case, General Vipsanius is boxed in on all four sides. This is going to be bloody. There's nowhere he can run. He has no choice but to fight with his back up against the wall."

"Then let's send him and his men to hell," Oadira nodded. "Order the men to advance now. Tell them I will be with them every step."

"Yes, my queen."

Despite General Vipsanius's dwindling numbers, he

seemed to realize the citizens of Iceoth wanted to wipe him out entirely, leaving no witans alive. That being the case, his forces pushed back all the harder, eventually breaking through and advancing on Oadira's position.

"Shield wall," Oadira yelled out as a legion of colonials charged the hill she was using to gauge her battle strategies. A shield wall of soldiers nine levels deep lined up to protect their queen.

"Squeeze them!" Oadira yelled.

All four sides of the Iceoth army pushed forward at her command and started killing witans with optimum efficiency. Soldiers fought with exquisite precision, opening their shield wall to kill the general's men repeatedly. When they fell, their bodies became the ground beneath the warrior's feet, and their blood drenched the white snow scarlet red. The box grew smaller and smaller as the colonial army dwindled to nothing more than a few hundred surviving men. Even so, Oadira did not relent.

"Repel!" yelled Oadira.

The four sides of the shield wall stopped simultaneously and backed up at least a feet away from General Vipsanius's men.

"Sky shield," Oadira cried.

Ossa ordered the archers to fire arrows into the center of the shield wall, killing many more of the general's men.

"Open up!" Oadira ordered.

The shield wall opened, allowing the cavalry to attack from all four angles, taking out more of the general's men.

"Four corners and squeeze!" yelled Oadira. "I am going to send a message to General Vipsanius and the colonies that Iceoth is permanently off-limits."

The battle went on until the first rays of morning made

their way over the frozen land from the eastern sea.

Eventually Oadira could see the faces of her enemy as less than a dozen colonial soldiers remained. And there in the center of them was General Vipsanius. He had long brown hair and wore the armor of an elevated soldier. Yellow teeth grit tight against his pale flesh. He looked dirty and tired but retained the danger of a cornered animal ready to fight to the death.

She remembered seeing him once before at the Royal Rumble over a year and a half before. He had been so haughty and superior as he sat next to President Tiberius of Trienneum and Natas himself. Now he looked like half a man, bloodied and beaten, ready to bite the first thing that came into his view.

"Open!" Oadira ordered. The sound of swords clanging against each other ceased.

"Allow me to enter for you, my queen," Ossa said. "There is no need to put yourself in danger now."

"You may stand by my side, Ossa," Oadira replied. "But you will not stand in my way, whether to protect me or otherwise."

Ossa nodded and stepped aside.

The shield wall opened, allowing Oadira to walk into the center with Ossa next to her. Vipsanius' soldiers crowded around him to protect their leader.

"You are all that remain of your great militia," Oadira said to General Vipsanius.

General Vipsanius looked at the forces squared around him, wiping blood from his lip. He stepped out from among his men, standing mere feet from Oadira.

"Stand down, forces of Iceoth. Drop your weapons," he spat. "As long as you're here, Oadira of Sahael, invasions will continue until you're all too weak to fight them off. The time will come when the people lose the will to fight, and when that day comes, all will surely die. My life doesn't matter so long as Lord Commander Natas has his prize. If I should fall, I will rise again to finish what I have started this day!"

Vipsanius raised his sword above his head and stepped toward Oadira like an attacking beast.

She didn't cower or sway in the slightest. Forming a sword of blue energy in her hand, she blocked his blow, pivoting to the right, and cutting General Vipsanius across the chest, exposing his vital organs. Before he had a chance to gasp his last breath, Oadira decapitated him. His head hit the ground before his body had a chance.

Oadira wiped General Vipsanius's blood from her sword on the man's own cape.

"Kill them all," she said softly, ordering the execution of the General Vipsanius's remaining troops.

The final slaughter began as Oadira stepped back past the shield wall with Ossa. The final surge lasted less than a minute before a cry of victory echoed through the valley.

"Our victory is not complete," Ossa whispered to Oadira as the soldiers cheered. "Look across the valley."

Oadira saw the Ennead army watched the celebration less than a mile away. It was the same group they had seen the day before along the ridge outside Benin. Large mammoths pulled wagons that Oadira recognized as those that had carried the dead bodies from the earlier battlefield.

"Why aren't they advancing?" Oadira asked.

"That looks like Commander-in-Chief Atum's flag with the Black symbol of Ankh on the leading detachment," Ossa said, pointing to a banner of yellow with a symbol similar to Natas'. "His nine Ennead commanders are likely with him."

A sound surged over the wind, mingling with the cheers of Iceoth soldiers. The sound built into a song with no words, hauntingly beautiful, but filling the soul with grief; a depressing song of love, darkness, and depression.

"Can you hear that?" Oadira asked.

"Hear what?" Ossa replied.

"The song of the dead. The dead have started to sing Nova's Song."

Ossa shook his head. "I can't hear anything."

I fear before the day is done," Oadira said, "we'll all be hearing the song."

CHAPTER III

THE CARRIERS OF THE DEAD

Aarde, Iceoth, The Clearing

For the next few hours, the Ennead didn't move from their position on the edge of the clearing. The Nethanite Body Retrievers, Nethanite priests, and Ennead soldiers in black robes tasked with the removal of the dead after combat, wandered the battlefield collecting corpses. They loaded dead bodies onto the carts and brought them back to the Ennead. Once the wagons were full, a portal of red and black energy opened up, large enough for the mammoths to walk through, followed by the carts full of the dead.

"What's happening?" Oadira asked.

"The Nethanites are collecting the dead," Ossa said.

"Is this normal? They're coming closer with each pass. Will they attack us?" Oadira questioned, watching the Nethanites as they began pulling bodies from immediately next to the Iceoth soldiers on her left flank. "And what of the Ennead. They're just standing there, not attacking."

“Don’t draw any of your weapons, just let them go about their business,” Ossa suggested. “I’m not sure why they’re taking them through Nebuchadnezzar’s Portal, or where they’re going, but they won’t attack us. They are doing the jobs of what the Demirrians used to do. We just have to allow them to do their work.”

“Who has the power to open a portal that big?” Oadira asked. She had never seen a temporal rift that large before. It had to require a massive will and understanding of magic artes.

The Nethanites continued to load dead bodies of soldiers from both sides into the wagons. They even took the body of General Vipsanius. As they passed, several of them looked at Oadira, faces expressionless.

“Queen! My queen!” A soldier shouted behind Oadira. The young man came running up to her out of breath, afro splattered with blood, though he seemed uninjured.

“What is it, soldier?” she asked.

“Steward Nilhist asks for you. He is injured.”

Oadira and Ossa followed the young soldier across the meadow, passing families of refugees who shivered in the cold, but smiled warmly and waved as Oadira passed. Many of them shouted thanks for her leadership.

Nilhist stood with a group of generals in torn capes and dented armor. His left side was bandaged, and his beard looked grayer than it ever had before, but he seemed in good health otherwise.

“Oadira,” he said with a nod. “We are victorious for now. But the Ennead are taking all the bodies, and I don’t know why. These soldiers of Iceoth deserve a proper burial, not to be taken and desecrated by our enemies.”

“We don’t know what they’re doing with the bodies,”

Oadira replied. "I suggested we investigate. They didn't come armed, so we allowed them to pass, but you're right, these are our people, and their families deserve to see them, not some invading army."

"Finding out why at a later time would be best," Ossa cautioned. "The two of you may not need rest, but the rest of us do. Our men are exhausted. They didn't even put up a fight when the Nethanites came to take their brothers because they are too tired to fight anymore."

Nilhist agreed and the group retreated to a tent that had been sent up on the outskirts of the forest. He told them that he fought First Commander Shu of the ennead legion, and that his opponent was the most powerful person with whom he had ever clashed. He said the commander could have killed him but chose not to, and he wondered why.

"Something is happening that we don't comprehend," Nilhist said. "They know you are here, Oadira. Either they are waiting for a greater force to arrive on our shores, or they are afraid of you. Either way, our respite will be short."

So many questions Oadira needed answering, and it seemed that for every solution she discovered, six more mysteries manifested.

As she pondered, recognizing for the first time in 12 hours just how tired she truly was, a cheer rose up outside the tent.

"What's going on?" Nilhist asked one of his guards. "Go find out."

Before the soldier could leave the tent, the flap flew open and in stepped Lyshyla with a broad grin.

"Lyshyla!" Oadira said. "What happened in the forest? Did you find Ozias?"

"Honestly, I did not, my queen," Lyshyla said, smile as big

as ever. "Because he found me."

Another cheer rose up from the soldiers outside, and King Ozias stepped into the tent, face dirty, blood smeared on his tunic, a sword in his hand.

"Ozias!" Oadira rushed forward and embraced her husband. They kissed and held each other close.

"What happened?" Nilhist asked, face pale as if he'd just received good news beyond all hope. "We feared we would never see you again."

"You're not that lucky, Father," Ozias said, smiling as broadly as Lyshyla. "Once the sirens took Oadira, the Anubis Guard and I made shelter for ourselves. By morning we began our trek once again, only to find ourselves trapped between the Colonial Army and a mass of refugees being steered toward the clearing as bait for a battle. By the time we made it back through the forest, the battle had already begun, and we joined in on the eastern edge, keeping any wayward soldiers from escaping."

"You fought?" Oadira asked, tears in her eyes.

"Nothing as dramatic as you, my dear. All I've been hearing all morning is how Queen Oadira has saved the people and killed the leader of the colonials herself. I'm jealous, to tell you the truth. Now, where are our sons? You run into battle the day after giving birth to triplets? I get left behind for a few hours and madness takes over."

"Well, it's time to make sure she remains safe along with my grandchildren," former King Nilhist said. "With your permission, son, Oadira is to be heavily guarded and placed on constant watch along with your children for as long as you remain in Iceoth."

King Ozias agreed his family should be heavily guarded and kept away from the surface until all the remnants of the colonial forces and the Ennead were no longer lurking about the continent for dead soldiers.

"Let's gather up the wounded and get back to the caverns as soon as we can," Queen Oadira ordered.

The men, women, and children greeted their king and queen as the mass of soldiers and evacuees returned to the hidden refuge. They were happy about being saved from the invading colonial forces of Lucedale. The queen's guards and midwives watched over their children, but Oadira was overjoyed to hold each of them in the comforts of their cavernous room. She had snuggled her boys for only a brief time while breastfeeding them before going off to battle, and now that the call of war had quieted, she sat with Ozias, content in a cave as if it had been the most sumptuous palace in Aarde. They slept, ate, and enjoyed a day of quiet repose.

Have you come up with names for the boys? Ozias telepathically asked Oadira as he wrapped a blanket around her shoulders and joined her next to a small fireplace carved into the cave wall where a warm blaze glowed.

No, I wanted you to be the one to name your male children, Oadira smiled. *It's tradition in Iceoth, isn't it?*

New traditions are going to have to be reestablished where you and I will all have an equal say in what we name our children. You did just lead our armies into battle, something no queen has ever done before. It's a new precedent. I truly do love you, King Ozias said, his mind softly caressing Oadira's.

And I love you, my king. I'm truly blessed that you have turned up in my life at the time you did.

I feel the same way, my love. The Signs of the Times are upon us. Speaking of which; why do you think the Ennead were taking all the dead bodies?

I don't know, Oadira admitted. *It's strange. To take the dead of your own soldiers is honorable, but all the dead no matter who they are or how they died? It makes no sense.*

Perhaps tomorrow we can go to the archives in the pyramid and see what we can learn.

Lyshyla entered their private quarters through the cloth barrier hanging over the entrance and slowly approached the royal couple.

"I can see that you both are communicating telepathically now," Lyshyla said.

"How do you know?" Ozias asked.

Lyshyla smiled. "The minute your eyes locked onto each other during the wedding ceremony, it connected the both of you for time and eternity. That's a bond not easily formed, and not easily broken. In over twenty-four months, the two of you have become a beacon of hope for the Orishan people. In fact, many of them wish to see you and the crown princes. This evening I suggest you come to the throne room and eat with the regents and gathered masses. Everyone is overjoyed at yesterday's victory. There is still unease but hope springs even in the dark recesses of these caves."

That night Oadira and Ozias entered the throne room with a group of midwives carrying the newborn boys. While not as opulent as the destroyed palace of Benin, the cave had been carved expertly with arched ceilings and torched along the walls. They were greeted and celebrated by the population due to the amazing feat they had just accomplished. King Ozias and Queen Oadira mingled among the Iceoth people, laughing and smiling despite their concerns of the Ennead collecting the bodies of the dead for unknown reasons.

After the festivities concluded, Oadira and Ozias asked his stepfather and Lyshyla to meet them in their chambers.

"Who are these Ennead?" Ozias asked the moment the last chambermaid tied the cloth door closed upon her exit. Nilhist and Lyshyla shook their heads.

"They were a part of Natas' force the day he overthrew Sahael," Oadira answered.

"Yes, they're one of his armies," Ozias nodded. "But why weren't they attacking, and why were they gathering all the bodies? The man in black had to be here for a reason. It's best we find out what the reason is. You said father that he was believed to be the son of Natas?"

"That is one theory," Nilhist nodded. "It is said that after the fall of Sahael, the son of Natas, Damien, was sent by his father to comb Aarde for the four missing princesses. He wore a cloak so dark no light could escape it. He never found the princess but is said to search even now. His eyes are orange and his skin dark as night, like his cloak."

"Orange eyes…" Oadira whispered, remembering siting with her cousins behind Natas as a man in a mysterious black cloak that seemed to absorb the light whispered to the Lord Commander before staring at Oadira, Heziara, and Aamira. He had orange eyes.

"What is it?" Ozias asked.

"How you describe this man in black reminds me of the man we encountered in the coliseum of El Djem," Oadira said, "It was only for a moment, but he made direct eye contact with my cousins and I, looking us straight in the eyes. I remember his orange eyes and that Aamira said how she felt the chills when he looked at us. Could this be the same man?"

"Events are happening all over Aarde," Lyshyla answered. "If this is Damien, the son of Natas, he chose this place due to the colonial guards reporting to their superiors about your presence here, Oadira. Tell me more about your encounter with Lord Commander Natas. Do you remember anything else that could help us?"

"No," Oadira admitted.

"What else happened that day?" Lyshyla asked.

"That's when my sisters and I met Solomon, who had carefully orchestrated setting up a meeting with us. He explained to us our history and provided us with a plan of escape to the outer lands."

"But why didn't the Ennead attack yesterday?" Ozias questioned. "They were outnumbered by the end, but if they had joined the fray earlier, they may have turned the tide in the colonial's favor. Why hold back?"

"I think they're afraid," Nilhist said, nodding his head. He pointed at Oadira. "You led the army from the south. You were on the field. The prophesies of the power of the lost princesses are known by the Ennead. In fact, to them they're not prophesies; they're promises."

"I disagree," Lyshyla said. "I am older than I look, and I know more than I let be known. I think the Ennead performed the exact duty they were sent here to perform: collect the bodies of the dead. Nothing more, nothing less."

Ozias got up and walked around the room. "Whatever the case, we bought ourselves some time with yesterday's victory. It's best to use that bought time to heal our wounded and learn what we must. Oadira and I, with your help Lyshyla, must read through Iceoth histories. If we do this, we can find the answers to our questions. And you, Lyshyla, need to tell us what you know but have not let be known. The time for riddles has passed."

Lyshyla took a deep breath. "I'll teach you what you need to know throughout our time together. Keep in mind, Iceoth's history is rich, and most of it was hidden away when Sahael fell. All that history is in a safe location that houses the records of Aarde in Timbuktu. Searching through the archives within our great pyramid will provide some answers as well. I'll point you in the right direction when I know where you should be looking. For now, go enjoy the day and get your rest and spend time with your family. Your father and I will get everyone situated in the next couple of weeks. We'll have a council meeting tomorrow with the regents and spies, so we know the movement of the enemy on our shores."

Ozias nodded in agreement. "It should be noted that the priority is to search for solutions on what to do next. There is over four hundred years of history in that pyramid. We're going to be there for a while."

"And after that," Oadira said slowly, "I fear our path will lead us away from this land. Sahael is calling to me, and I will answer."

The next few weeks were a whirlwind of activity. Spies reported to the council that the remaining colonial ships had fled Iceoth, leaving behind several fine vessels that no longer had enough men to sail them. They had been confiscated and were being used to attack enemy ships on the open waters. The colonial army had been decimated in the sneak attack in the clearing at the feet of Mount Arrion, and since then, no new forces had landed. The Ennead had cleared the land of bodies, and still, no one understood why.

Nilhist had decided that once Oadira and Ozias found what they were looking for in the pyramid archives, he would be staying in Iceoth with a small percentage of the people to ensure the bloodline was kept intact and hidden. If Oadira and Ozias needed to leave to reclaim Sahael, then fine, but he would stay. Nilhist also confirmed that he would continue taking in refugees from off the ships and would nurse them back to health, helping them get strong and rebuild the cities before rebuilding the army to protect the island.

The king agreed with his stepfather, as did Oadira. Nilhist would assume control of the continent when Sahael is made whole, and once again rein as King of Iceoth. Nilhist spent much time with his son, Oadira, and Lyshyla over the passing weeks before leaving to the surface for the ruins of Benin City.

"I am sorry I kept so many secrets for far too long," he said as he mounted a kelpy on a fine late summer morning. "Find a way to learn about the Nairohenge, and Nabtahenge Gates. They are the key to helping you get Sahael restored.

"Where are they located?" Lyshyla asked. "We can't find anything in the archives. It's been months now. What did you learn before those records were returned to Timbuktu when Ozias was born?"

"They were buried somewhere within this cavern," Nilhist said. "I never looked for them beyond the basic knowledge of their use. I was angry. My people came to this frozen land from Sahael. We were Orishan. And yet, we were forgotten by our people as one forgets a bad dream. I felt abandoned and thus had no desire to ever unite with Sahael again. I do remember that the information was made available to the Kemettian bloodline in the stories I heard when Ozias was a little child. The information wasn't sent to Timbuktu and thus remains somewhere in the pyramid archives. It just needs to be rediscovered."

He rode off into a blue-sky morning with a collection of Anubis guards. That evening Oadira, Ozias, and Lyshyla agreed they would study day and night until they found the gates and any details they could about Natas and his son. They tended to the growing boys, taking turns watching them as Oadira breastfed her sons.

They still didn't have names.

That fact didn't bother Oadira. Their names would come to her and Ozias when they were meant to, and when they had meaning. For now, they were merely 'the boys,' or as Ozias liked to call them, 'the brood.'

Months passed, and once again, colder weather descended on Iceoth as winter fell. The caverns and pyramid remained at a more or less consistent temperature, but when Oadira would venture outside to harvest sweet grasses with the people, she could tell another harsh season approached.

The children continued to be a distraction, now running around, and knocking books off shelves as the royal couple continued pouring through the books in the archive. One afternoon the three toddlers knocked over a large pile of books that Oadira hadn't gotten to yet, creating a mess on the floor.

"Ozias!" she called, voice echoing around the shelves and bouncing off the high ceiling. "Can you please come get the boys? They're distracting me, and I just found a passage that I'm interested in."

No response.

Oadira rolled her eyes. Ozias was probably making dinner with Ossa.

Oadira stood from her chair and walked over to her sons, who were pushing the books over, seeming to enjoy the sound they made as they thumped against the tile floor. A blue glow emanated from one of the books, which caught Oadira by surprise. Even more shocking for her, the boys' eyes were glowing blue as well.

She ran and found Lyshyla and Ozias immediately.

They examined the book together. It was large, leather-bound and was sealed with three small handprints on it linked to a metal clasp. The outside of the book had an image of the Nabtahenge Gates, volcanic glass obelisks that formed a circle.

"How do we open it?" Ozias asked.

"The children are the only ones that could've found the book," Lyshyla said. "They are obviously linked to it. Look at their eyes. They glow sapphire like the book. They are the only ones who can remove the seal."

"When did the book start glowing?" Ozias questioned, running his fingers along the metal clasp and handprints. "It wasn't yesterday. I passed that pile of books, thinking I would start reading them within the next few days, but there was no blue glow."

Oadira caressed the hand of one of her children and smiled. "It started radiating the sapphire hue when the boys touched it. This is a sign."

They each grabbed the left hands of the babies and placed them onto the empty hand slots of the book. A spinel mist came out of the book, enveloping them all and penetrating the minds of every royal family member. Oadira could hear Ozias' thoughts as if they were communicating telepathically, but she could also feel the emotions of her sons, and their playful curiosity. Even Lyshyla's mind was open to her. Images appeared in her mind of tunnels, underwater caverns, and the silhouette of rectangular stones standing in a circular pattern with rocky crossbeams, opening up a portal to Sahael.

“Did you see that?” Ozias breathed.

“Yes,” Lyshyla nodded.

“I did as well,” Oadira confirmed. “This is the book we’ve been searching for. This is our way back to Sahael!”

CHAPTER IV

THE NAIROHENGE GATES

Iceoth, The Pyramid

"According to the book, and the images we all saw when the mist surrounded us, the Nibiru tunnels lead off from somewhere south of the pyramid," Lyshyla said as Oadira rocked the last of her boys to sleep before placing him in a bassinet beside his brothers.

Ozias leaned over the table, taking the last few bites of kelpie meat from what remained of their dinner. "Is there a map or anything more specific? Some the uncharted caverns go for miles into the dark, and no one knows whether they dead-end or continue all the way to the ocean."

"Much of the writing is in Egyptian," Lyshyla said. "The hieroglyphic symbols are a bit different than I'm used to, but I think I'm getting an understanding of what the text is trying to convey. I'm reading about these Nairohenge Gates and their function now."

"What have you learned?" Oadira asked.

"Some of it I know already, but some is…new. The

Nairohenge gates have a dangerous history associated with them," Lyshyla said, flipping pages. "According to this book, the Ukáváál designed them to achieve their objective of spreading White Darkness all over Kolob, the original home of our Kemite ancestors. The Ukáváál forced the ancient Kemites to help build the Nairohenge Gates all over their world as part of an agreement to live in peace, so their children weren't...What is this symbol? Eaten? Yes, it says eaten."

"Eaten?" Oadira asked. "Were the Ukáváál cannibals?"

"According to this, they were cannibals but not for reasons you might think. It doesn't say much, but the ancients seemed to do whatever the Ukáváál wanted." Lyshyla paused for a moment to take a breath. She seemed disturbed.

"What's wrong?" Oadira asked.

"It says here that a porcelain man named Urák was born out of hate on the planet of Kolob, an intelligent, mechanical being covered in flesh and blood. In order to stay alive, Urák needed a spirit to activate the flesh in his body. He was the first to create the Ukáváál. Urák arrived on a planet full of Black people and for no reason at all wanted to whitewash their rich and extensive history, ensuring that a sentient race of porcelain machines would rule the planet."

One of the boys wined for a moment and Oadira rocked the bassinet back and forth quickly, hoping the children would remain asleep.

"I read about the Ukáváál in some of the archive books when Ozias and I first started looking for ways to reach Sahael," Oadira whispered as the child quieted down. "It's said they destroyed Kolob, but there were no details about their origins or this Urák individual."

Lyshyla ran her finger down the pages of the book, eyes

darting back and forth as she read. "According to this, Urák split himself into two different people, creating Uráék, his wife."

"Interesting way to procreate," Ozias said, chewing another piece of meat. "Not how I'd want to do it, but..."

Lyshyla looked at him silently, but her eyes told him to keep his comments to himself. "The two of them could reproduce their own offspring through their jade stones," she continued, "created by using scolecite mist capable of turning ordinary stones into jade stones. They filled these stones with White Darkness. They lived in a large, expansive...I think it says hollow or grotto, like a cave where you had to travel underwater to get inside. It was full of tunnels penetrating the solid rock and extending thousands of miles inside the mountains that covered the planet of Kolob. Urák discovered that Uráék's empty mechanical vessel needed a Dybbuk rejected spirit to sustain her mechanical mind."

"What's a Dybbuk spirit?" Ozias asked.

"I don't know. It doesn't say. Perhaps as we read through their history, we can deduce what it might be. The children of Urák needed to find a way to keep their flesh fresh and safe from falling from their mechanical bodies. It was no use to them to multiply if they couldn't keep from decaying."

"So, what did they do?" Oadira asked.

Lyshyla turned the book and showed Oadira and Ozias a painted image of pale, half-mechanical, decaying creatures clubbing rats, bats, and other beasts of the underground.

"This wood-carved image says it all. Urák and Uráék resorted to killing the cave animals. It helped a little but ultimately couldn't keep their flesh safe, forcing it to rot. So, to save his wife, the first thing he did was kidnap an ancient Kemite man who was drowning and brought him down into their water cave. His mechanical body performed a scan of the man's muscles and organs, revealing that the man had both elements they needed to not only survive but to also grow and multiply. Urák used the white jade stones by cracking one and allowing scolecite mist to infect the Kemite man's mind, forcing his body to reject its spirit and breaking up the man's soul, killing him. Urák took the Dybbuk spirit and placed it inside of Uráék's body, allowing her to live eternally."

"Is this legend or history?" Oadira asked, taking her seat next to Lyshyla once more.

"A little of both, I would assume, but I'm sure it's more historical than we would care to admit."

"What happened to their flesh? Did it continue to rot?" Ozias questioned.

"No, Urák, the first Ukáváál, resorted to cannibalism, which allowed his porcelain skin to stay fresh as long as a consistent stream of bodies were available. Urák and Uráék supported their growing family by ambushing travelers in the forest next to the mountains connected to the villages; the bodies provided a high protein diet of meat for the Ukáváál. Over two decades, generations of Ukáváál were replicated, refining their skills of murder and cannibal cuisine, including the art of…I assume I'm reading this right…salting and pickling their flesh."

Ozias pushed the plate with what remained of their meal across the table and coughed.

"What did the ancient Kemite leaders do about this?" Oadira asked.

"I know this part of the story from my own studies in Timbuktu," Lyshyla answered. "The former ancient Kemite leaders Hemiunu and Khay were made aware of the missing Kemites and wanted to find out how they were disappearing. Hundreds of Kemites disappeared, forcing the ancient Kemite leaders of Kolob to review the list of missing persons. Khay, the wife of Hemiunu, organized mass searches of the areas where the Kemites were kidnapped. They never thought to search inside of the mountainous caves."

Lyshyla continued reading the book for a moment before she spoke again. "It says here Urák and Uráék's family continued to grow in number, and so did their appetites. As many as 500 Kemites were abused and kidnapped at a time in military style operations by the Ukávááł army. Their bodies were taken back to their secret cave to be carefully prepared for consumption by those responsible for placing jade stones next to the incapacitated victims. Afterward, they released the scolecite, infecting their bodies, taking the rejected Dybbuk spirits to bring life to more Ukávááł. After that, they would skin the bodies down to the bone to keep their porcelain flesh refreshed."

"How were they eventually discovered?" Oadira asked.

"Although they were calculating creatures, they were exposed one evening as the Ukávááł army attacked Hemiunu and Khay, who were out looking for clues of the kidnapped victims. One group of Ukávááł ambushed them, taking a man from their entourage, stripping him, and disemboweling him before them, while kidnapping Khay. The Ukávááł, realizing that fate was about to fall upon them, fought desperately to escape, using Khay to lure Hemiunu into their domain to help them take over Kolob. As Urák and Uráék fought for their lives, a group of fifty Kemites following behind Hemiunu and Khay happened upon the scene. After a brief and violent exchange, the Urák and Uráék found themselves for the first time ever at a numerical disadvantage and promptly retreated to the Urúk mountains to consider their situation. As they retreated, they left behind the mutilated body of the man as evidence, along with hundreds of witnesses and angry people."

"What happened to the Khay and Hemiunu?" Oadira asked,

sitting forward. The thought of being taken by such a depraved enemy made her skin crawl.

Taking a deep breath, Lyshyla continued. "This part of the story I know as well, without the help of the book. It is a great tragedy from our ancient history. Rather than killing and consuming Hemiunu and Khay, Urák and Uráék infected their hearts with hate, infusing them with untold amounts of scolecite. It made their insides like the Ukáváál, sentient and mechanical, and in need of flesh to allow them to keep their bodies of skin and blood, essentially upgrading the Ukáváál as a people. Khay and Hemiunu became their new leaders. Urák and Uráék became their servants and military leaders. Together they devised a plan to save their new people.

Emotion became evident on Lyshyla's face. "The Kemites were…devastated. Kaimana and Kanoa became Khay and Hemiunu's replacements and used four hundred warriors with several packs of tracker dogs and a band of locals from the area to search for their fallen leaders. It was one of the biggest manhunts the planet had ever seen."

"What happened next?" Ozias asked.

Lyshyla returned to the book, as if hiding her sadness behind the pages of the ancient manuscript. She flipped several leaves ahead and continued her translation. "Kaimana and Kanoa abandoned the search to attend to other matters, ordering the army to find and kill all Ukáváál. The army searched throughout the mountainside, the countryside, and the coastline, but like before, discovered nothing. That was, however, until their dogs picked up the scent of decaying Kemite flesh while passing a partly waterlogged cave."

"The Ukáváál hunt was closing in!" Ozias said. Never before had history engrossed her so. Even Solomon's tales in his tent at the Royal Rumble hadn't captured her imagination like this.

"Yes, using torchlight, the Kemite troops entered the Ukúl caves and withdrew Ikakalaka swords. They proceeded down the miles-long, twisting passages to the inner depths of the Ukáváál lair."

Again, Lyshyla turned the book, revealing another wood-carved image with painted accents. This one showed dozens of dead bodies on a cave floor while men with torches stood at the entrance. Severed arms and legs hung from the walls like a butcher's display.

"The damp walls of the cave were strewn with Kemite limbs and body parts," Lyshyla continued. "The Ukáváál had hundreds of areas in the cave where bundles of clothing, piles of jade rocks, and skulls and heaps of discarded bones from previous feasts existed. Hold on," Lyshyla paused. "Some of the symbols are smudged here. I think it's saying the soldiers walked into a large room of nothing except broken jade stones, which filled the room with scolecite mist. It was a trap. Hemiunu and Khay were in the center of the cavern as their Kemite armies were sacrificed to help awaken more of the replicated Ukáváál, allowing them to spread White Darkness all over the planet of Kolob."

"What happened to Urák and Uráék?" Ozias asked.

"They upgraded their bodies to match those of Khay and Hemiunu and ruled Kolob by their side, using the people on the planet as a food source, body part supply, and labor force. They ordered their scouts to look for more worlds they could devour, knowing their resources were finite and would die if they didn't find another place to support their growing race."

"Do we know if they made it here to Aarde?" Oadira asked. The memory of the Ennead collecting bodies at the end of the battle suddenly sprung to her mind.

"It goes on to say that the Kemite leaders, Kanoa and Kaimana, came up with a plan to save their people from the

Ukáváál," Lyshyla said.

"You're avoiding my question," Oadira pressed.

Lyshyla's eyes narrowed a bit, but she nodded. "Let's finish here first before we start making assumption as toi whether they're here on Aard or not. The text says Kanoa and Kaimana made a treaty with the Ukáváál, where they helped design and construct the Nairohenge Gates all over the planet Kolob. They built a large circle, and inside of the circle, they constructed fifteen gates and four singular inner gates. After designing them, the Ukáváál ordered them to test them to determine if they were operational."

"So, the ancient Kemites built the gates for the Ukáváál?" Oadira asked. "This is crazy! So, the Ukáváál are the source of the White Darkness? I heard Solomon speak of this whiteness here on Aarde. He mentioned that it has infected the witans and that it will spread to all witans in time. If that's the case, the Ukáváál have to be here."

"The Ukáváál used it to erase history," Lyshyla confirmed. "At the very least, their influence has survived. They wanted to appear as if they were the superior race; when, in actuality, it was a delusion of grandeur. There are a few side notes here and there beside the drawings that mention how the Ukáváál understood their unnatural existence, which pushed them to prove their superiority."

"How did they accomplish the erasing of history?" Ozias asked.

"According to what I've read, the Ukáváál single-handedly destroyed all of the other civilizations, whitewashing their history and culture, due to the fact they had no culture or history of their own," Lyshyla said.

"I can see why the ancient Kemites did as they were

ordered; they were cautious about having their history entirely erased," Oadira said.

"That's right. As a result, they figured out how to operate the Nairohenge Gates. The ancient Kemites were able to activate the thirteenth, fourteenth, and fifteenth gates within the henge circle. They used dark matter to power the gates. In fact, all the dark matter in Kolob was required to power these three individual gates. In secret, due to desperation, they activated one of the dark doors, entering through it and arriving in Aarde as it was being formed by Ishtar and Obatala. Apparently Kanoa and Kaimana explained their situation to Ishtar and Obatala, who were preparing to shape the world of Aarde in their own image. They agreed to allow the Kemite leaders to live and dwell in Aarde before they added plant life, water, and animals of all sorts. Ishtar and Obatala gave Kanoa and Kaimana the coordinates to travel to Aarde through space."

"So, that's how they came to be in Aarde," Oadira said. "That's how the vessel that looked like an asteroid crashed and how all of us came to be."

"Just like that they, gave the coordinates to come to Aarde?" Ozias asked. "If Ishtar and Obatala knew about the Ukáváál, wouldn't they have wanted to keep their creation safe from them?"

Lyshyla flipped through the pages and read for a few minutes as Oadira and Ozias sat silently. Only the breathing fo the sleeping boys could be heard beyond the turning of pages.

"Kaimana and Kanoa were asked if they would look over the Black inhabitants of Aarde, as part of the agreement for allowing them to take refuge in their created world," Lyshyla said, looking back up at the king and queen. "Ishtar and Obatala wanted to give the people of Aarde the ability to use free will. They knew and understood that others would object to having free will and would try to convince them to give up their agency to live a certain way, safe, but without choice."

"Free will?" Ozias asked.

"The ability to choose a life of their own without being coerced in any way whatsoever," Lyshyla nodded. "Ishtar and Obatala wanted to provide a savior that would redeem the people of their sins and allow them to grow into eternal beings like they were."

"Who were they going to send?" Oadira asked.

Turning the book toward them yet again, Lyshyla showed an image of a man with long dreadlocks and dark skin, arms outstretched, with shafts of light emanating from his chest and abdomen.

"Horus was to be the savior they had chosen to redeem the people of Aarde," Lyshyla said, pointing at the image. "Ishtar and Obatala knew it would upset others in Andalusia and needed a contingency to keep Horus safe until he redeemed the people of Aarde to have their souls saved. Kaimana and Kanoa agreed to Ishtar and Obatala's set of conditions. Reentering the thirteenth gate, they arrived back in Kolob, informing their people of haven," Lyshyla said, turning the book back toward herself. "Kaimana and Kanoa explained after returning that they could be safe and out of harm's way. Their elder leaders, Pharaohs, Ptolemies' and viziers wanted to live without the fear of White Darkness whitewashing their minds and personal history. They feared being part of a cultureless race of uncaring violent beings who cared for nothing except hate, anger, and death.

"This says here that Kaimana and Kanoa came up with a plan that could get them all to Aarde safely. It involved having to travel through the gorgeous blackness of space," Lyshyla said.

"Why didn't they use the thirteenth gate to get away from

the Ukáváál?" Oadira asked. "They used it once. Why not use it again?"

"Kanoa and Kaimana knew that if they left, they'd be followed through the thirteenth gate, knowing that the Ukáváál would do the same and might bring destruction to their world of refuge," Lyshyla said. "Kaimana and Kanoa came up with a solution, choosing to keep the gate technology to themselves, knowing that it would make the Ukáváál too powerful. They knew that with Nairo's technology, the Ukáváál could travel to any planet and whitewash it as they did in their own home world.

"The Kemite leaders then destroyed the gate. They broke it into little pieces, knowing that whatever it touched would activate them. So, Nairo made sure that it wouldn't fall into the hands of the Ukáváál. They agreed to continue building Nairohenge Gates, buying themselves more than enough time to come up with a plan that involved sneaking away with Nairo's gate technology.

"It says here that Kaimana and Kanoa had their people work to steal one of Nyathera's asteroids and avoiding one of Njen's comets."

"Who's Njen?" Oadira asked.

"It says that Njen created comets filled with White Darkness. They were designed to travel in the gorgeous darkness of space for centuries until they made impact with a planet, alerting the Ukáváál of another civilization that could be whitewashed by the White Darkness, as the asteroid creates a dent inside of the planet upon impact, White Darkness spews out, infecting the animals, insects, and the ground—the entire planet.

"The Kemite leaders were able to acquire one of Nyathera's asteroids that was a part of the rotation to send out into the darkness of space. Nyathera retrofitted the asteroid with the entire Kemettian bloodline, consisting of one hundred million Kemites. Nyathera created cryotubes that would put the people in a state of hibernation to save their eternal lives until the asteroid hit where it was designated to hit.

"While working on the gates, it says that Kemites were able to sneak onto one of Njen's asteroids during a war that they had created. It was a distraction in which they sacrificed a few for the many, allowing Nyathera to fly the asteroid off the planet without any signs of detection whatsoever." Lyshyla took a breath and grabbed the goblet next to their empty dinner plate and took a long drink.

Oadira sat back for a moment. Everything started to make sense now, from the cryptic words of Solomon, to the records she and Ozias had read the year before. These Ukávààl had destroyed everything…and could potentially do it all again.

"They did all of this to prevent Nairo's technology from falling into the wrong hands?" Oadira asked after their moment of silence.

"Yes," Lyshyla replied. "Nairo tied the gates to the Ancient Bloodline, preventing the Ukávààl from ever having any semblance of control of the gates. Nairo divided the Nairohenge Gates into thirds. He created Navigators, who were women who held one third of the power, to help anyone within the bloodline to travel through the gates safely to their desired destination. Elaborate designs were made into their hair, allowing them to travel freely in Aarde. They knew the Ukávààl would do all that was in their power to whitewash this aspect of their history."

Lyshyla laid the book on the table and flipped back several page to a painted image of a woman's scalp, where her hair had been braided in distinct patterns that could be interpreted as a map or instructions of some kind.

"I've seen these designs on the women in Madame Lalaurie's estate," Oadira said. "Days later they were gone though."

"The designs were also adapted and used to help runaways escape their enslavers," Lyshyla said candidly.

"You said the power was divided into thirds. What about the other two thirds of that power?" Ozias asked.

"The Medjay Gate Guardians were the other people who shared the power of the Nairohenge Gates. They were needed to help deal with threats as travel through the gates took place to keep travelers safe. They both were tied to the gates as the destroyed fragments were turned into small balls of volcanic rocks that were placed in the eyes of the Navigators and Medjay Gate Guardians. The irises of their eyes were black and gray, allowing the power of Nairohenge's Gates to activate and run through their blood," Lyshyla said.

"So, without the Navigators and the Medjay Gate Guardians, the gates cannot function properly?" Oadira asked.

"That's correct. It says that if they're not present or sense any threats, Nairo's gates will retract into the ground. Each Nairohenge at the top center had a piece of Nairo's original gate placed in it that would activate all of them in Aarde."

The discussion continued, but at this point, Oadira was aware of much of the history thanks to Solomon's teachings. Lyshyla continued explaining that Nyathera's asteroid broke off in multiple pieces, hitting in the center of Alkebulan, Egypt, Azteca, Ebony, and Rome Island, among other locations not named. Oadira and Ozias wanted to know more about the other locations where the asteroid hit, knowing that the center of the lands began floating in the skies with craters below them. The unnamed book refused to translate that section for reasons beyond their understanding; the spinel mist refused to interpret the emerald text.

Lyshyla skipped over the pages and continued reading the text.

"Damn. I want to know more about these floating islands. There was never any information regarding them in the libraries of Timbuktu, and I hoped we would find answers here. We will continue and read what we can, in any case. It says that when the ancients arrived, they created Nibiru tunnels in addition to the gates to avoid the sun, allowing travel over long distances as a contingency plan if the gates had to be shut down. The Nibiru tunnels connected to the five locations where Nyathera's asteroid pieces made impact with the five islands in Aarde, plus more locations that aren't recorded. But the Nairohenge Gates were all tied to Sahael and the five locations to ensure travel was always regulated and safe. According to this passage here, if Sahael were to regain access to the Nairohenge Gates, it would allow us the ability to have access to the other locations where Njen's asteroid hit."

"Whatever happened to these Ukáváál?" Oadira asked, nervous about the answer. The thought of half-dead, half-mechanical creatures chasing her unendingly brought a chill to her entire body.

"The Kemites were able to safely escape the Ukáváál, saving Aarde and their people from becoming another food source for them," Lyshyla said.

"How do we know that's true?" Oadira asked. "They left in their asteroid and never looked back. What if the Ukáváál found a way to escape?"

Lyshyla shook her head slowly. "We don't know…and will have to find out more when we get to Sahael. We've finished this section of the book, and it says nothing else of this history."

"What happened to Nairo?" Ozias asked. "The guy who created the gates in the first place?"

"No one knows," Lyshyla said, looking quickly at the floor before glancing back at Ozias.

She knew more than she was telling them, Oadira was certain.

"Did Ishtar and Obatala see a purpose for Nairo's gates?" Oadira asked, seeing if Lyshyla would again avoid the question.

"It was the main reason they were allowed to come to Aarde," Lyshyla confirmed. "Ishtar and Obatala wanted the ability to travel quickly to Aarde. The Ancient Elders helped create the four realms to make traveling easier between them, Andalusia, and the four realms of outer darkness. They agreed they could still worship their gods in Aarde; the Kemites just weren't allowed to worship them in Andalusia per the Nairobi laws."

Afterward, the spinel mist was no more, and the book was unreadable. Lyshyla kept the book with her at all times going forward, knowing she would one day need to pass it along to another Educator.

In the meantime, since learning about the hidden underwater tunnels that could lead them to the Iceoth gate, Oadira, Ozias, and Lyshyla spent most of their time searching the caverns surrounding the pyramid. Using the existing maps, they quickly discovered dozens of side tunnels that were uncharted.

They searched and looked around the caverns for weeks, noticing entrances blocked by stone and ice.

"Is it possible to search elsewhere?" Oadira asked after an arduous day of moving rocks around these blocked entrances.

"The access cavern to the tunnels was destroyed and covered up with large debris and rocks, frozen over in icestone," Lyshyla said. "This wasn't an accident. Someone wanted to keep anyone from accessing this tunnel. I would bet we've found what we're looking for."

"How long will it take to clear out all of this debris?" Oadira asked.

“It’ll take months to clear a path, with no time to waste,” Lyshyla said.

They summoned the guards and instructed them to help remove the rocks, debris, and icestone, to determine what they had found.

CHAPTER V

THE AWAKENING OF THE CHOSEN BLOODLINE

Iceoth, The Caverns

Months transformed into years. Work on the tunnel was slow, as whoever had sealed them originally had been diligent in making sure every inch had been packed with debris. Workers dug day in and day out, with only inches gained. By the end of five years, no one knew how much farther they had to dig, but they continued digging nonetheless.

Most of Icoeth's remaining population remained in the caverns surrounding the temple where food grew and animals grazed, but Steward Nilhist had succeeded in rebuilding parts of Benin City, along with other towns, so life began to return to the barren tundra of Iceoth.

No colonial army had attempted an invasion since their rout in the clearing of the valley of Arrion.

During this time of relative peace, Oadira would rotate between helping in the tunnels, harvesting berries for the winter stores, studying every book she could find in the archives, and listening as Lyshyla sat in the classroom, instructing her and Ozias' sons. The boys had grown inquisitive, listening intently as their instructor explained how the colonial invasion was won and the role Queen Oadira had played in winning the war.

"Wow, that's cool," Oya said.

"Yeah, cool," said Oshún.

"Indeed," Lyshyla said, smiling.

She turned around to face them after writing on the cement chalkboard.

"Your mother," she said, nodding toward Oadira as she sat across the room in a cushioned chair, "succeeded in luring forty thousand men out in the open, meeting them head-on on both sides, and beating them. She refused to let any of them leave Iceoth, knowing that General Vipsanius would come back. As a result, your mother killed him."

A hush fell over the usually rambunctious boys.

"What was your mother's phrase to justify his slaying of the general?" Lyshyla asked.

"It's far better for a single man to perish rather than a whole population, as is the Orishan way," all three boys repeated at the same time, making Lyshyla laugh.

"Our mother killed forty thousand colonial soldiers?" Oxum asked.

"Yes," Lyshyla said.

"All by herself?" Oxum added, glancing at his mother with awe on his face.

"Not by herself," Lyshyla confirmed. "Many brave men and women died in that battle protecting our people. Their souls are with Ishtar and Obatala."

"How many Orishans died?" Oshún asked.

"Over twenty-five thousand died during the Colonial Invasion," Lyshyla answered.

"Why did so many have to die?" Oxum asked.

"That's a lot of dead bodies. I wish I could've been there," Oya said.

"No you don't," Oadira interrupted. "A battle is not a good thing, and the death of any of our people is a tragedy. Sometime you may be called on to fight, my sons, but until then, don't glorify in it."

"What happened to the dead bodies?" Oya asked.

"The bodies were taken to Naharis's realm," Lyshyla said.

"Is there a reason why they took some bodies and left other bodies?" Oya asked.

"The Ennead now have the responsibility to carry the bodies of the dead to Naharis's realm. They chose to take this task over for reasons beyond our understanding," Lyshyla said.

"They took the dead to the Gates, right?" asked Oxum.

"Yes, I would assume so," replied Lyshyla.

"How many realms are there?" Oya asked.

"There are four realms in Aarde, and within each realm, resides one of Nebuchadnezzar's Portals, and then there are the actual gates. These gates allow those within Aarde access to the four portals within each of the realms located in the east, the north, the west, and the south," Lyshyla said.

"What purpose does each portal serve?" Oya asked.

"I haven't figured out the purpose of these portals yet," Lyshyla said. "You boys have become very good at asking questions. I'm sure your mother and father are very happy when it's my turn to provide the answers."

Lyshyla shook her head gently, got up, and started walking around the classroom. She unveiled Nephrophidas's map of Aarde from a rolled-up tapestry hanging from the far wall.

"Why are there three gates in northern Aarde and one gate in western Aarde?" Oya asked.

"Aarde was separated into two worlds, Eastern Aarde and Western Aarde, to keep an eye on Naharis's realm after the fall of Sahael separated it by Nibiru's wall. I'm still looking for answers. I have also yet to figure out the true purpose of the gates and their primary function in Aarde."

"What more can you tell us about the battle and our mom?" Oya asked.

"You boys and your interest in fame and glory," Lyshyla chuckled. "Such is the way of youth, I have found. Very well. The Queen used her Orishan artes, and her tattoos mysteriously lit up, creating an aura around her body and covering her from head to toe in Egyptus armor," Lyshyla explained, talking with her hands to emphasize armor covering a body.

The kids were in awe as Lyshyla told them of what had transpired. Oadira wanted to hug each of them but stayed back listening so as not to interrupt the lesson.

"Your mother was able to fight off thirty of General Vipsanius's soldiers," Lyshyla said, moving as if illustrating the battle. "Then she began fighting with General Vipsanius. Using her Orishan artes, she conjured up twin Ikakalaka long swords, enabling her to fight. The Ikakalaka were conjured up as blue outlines and took the form of real long swords."

"Wow!"

"Tell us more!"

"She battled with the general until the general had fallen to his knees, then your mother finished him off and ended the Colonial Invasion in Iceoth."

Oadira wanted to laugh out loud at the description. Lyshyla hadn't even been at the battle to witness any of this, since she had been tasked with finding Ozias in the forest. Still, the story had been told and retold so many times over the last five years that almost everyone in the kingdom could give the details Lyshyla now shared.

"Before killing General Vipsanius," she continued, "he asked how it was possible an Orishan woman such as your mother could have defeated his army."

"So, what happened next?" Oxum asked with a bold, serious look on his face.

"General Vipsanius asked your mother, 'Who are you?' And your mother stood tall for all to hear," Lyshyla said. "She said, 'I don't know, but my people have run and hid our whole lives, avoiding you at all costs. This is the last time you'll ever see Iceoth again.'"

The boys gasped in excitement as Lyshyla had them on the edge of their seats.

Again, Oadira almost laughed. Such embellishments had become common in this story, despite her having no memory of such an exchange between herself and General Vipsanius. History was becoming myth before her very eyes.

Lyshyla, for her part, continued to tell the tale with gusto. "The General looked up at your mother with blood trickling from his mouth and said, 'You have no idea of what you're up against. I am just a minor piece that has a part to play in bringing about permanent change. I'll rise to see you again one day before you die.' Before General Vipsanius could say more, your mother dealt him a killing blow and his body fell to the ground."

That last part was true. Oadira remembered it well, and his words continued to bring fear to her mind ever since she had learned of the Ukáváál. Would the general one day return as a mechanical, undying creature of pure hate? The thought now made her slightly queasy.

As Lyshyla finished the story, King Ozias appeared at the doorway.

Lyshyla looked up and clapped her hands. "That is enough for today, my young princes. Class dismissed. Go play before your training session. And stay out of the marshes where the harvest is taking place. Ossa told me you all caused some trouble with the other children last week. Mind your elders. Now go!"

"Awwww!" the boys moaned in unison.

"Not to worry. There is plenty of time to learn about the past," Lyshyla said, assuring them. "And to play in the warm marshes."

The boys stood up and chased each other out of the classroom.

"Wait up!" Oya yelled as Oxum and Oshún quickly excited the classroom.

Once the boys were out of sight, the king turned to Lyshyla, as she organized papers on the central stone table.

"They have lots of questions and are eager to learn more," he said, smiling at Oadira. "It's nice that they are being schooled by you. They are full of energy. It's a good thing they've got training today with Nilhist. That will drain them of all their energy."

"Indeed. What brings you here, my king?" Lyshyla asked. "Queen Oadira has been looking over my shoulder for the past hour as the boys questioned me about old battles. Do you also seek to check in on my teaching?"

"I'm here to see how much the story has changed over the past few years," Oadira grinned. "Nothing more."

"And I'm here for more serious matters," Ozias nodded. "Since the war, we've had multiple skirmishes with colonial threats on Iceoth's shores. They're looking for something. It's obvious. What are your thoughts?"

Lyshyla aimlessly fingered through ancient documents littered across the table before moving the papers from the king's reach and sitting down gently in her chair.

"I believe they'll continue to search all over Iceoth until they find Queen Oadira," Lyshyla said. "As long as the currents continue to bring colonial scouts to our shores, war will be a growing threat." She turned toward Oadira. "Natas knows you are here somewhere, my Queen. And the ice has been receding more each year. Soon, there will be no ice on Iceoth, which will be a strange occurrence indeed. This is why we must find a way to leave this place without exposing the people."

The king let out a heavy sigh and stared off into the distance.

"I need to figure out a way to get Oadira, the kids, and all the people out of Iceoth. The danger is getting worse. Sooner or later, we're going to slip up. Before that happens, I'd like to get out of here."

The weight of duty to his people and the imminent danger surrounding his wife and children seemed to weigh heavily on his shoulders. Oadira saw it day by day.

"My king, we must stay here until it's safe to travel," Lyshyla said softly. "Your wife is who they're looking for. Take comfort in knowing she's safe right here, and before long we'll get off this island."

The king gently stroked his well-groomed beard and inhaled sharply. "Good day" was all he said before he turned and disappeared out of the classroom.

"His burden grows," Oadira said as she stood and approached Lyshyla. "The work on the tunnel is slow. The raids increase. Ozias is a man of action. Waiting for something to happen is not how he would choose to live."

"And yet," Lyshyla replied, "we can do nothing but wait."

Just then, Ozias ran back into the room, with his best friend Ossa behind him.

"They broke through!" Ozias shouted excitedly. "Ossa caught me in the hallway. Tell them!"

Ossa, out of breath as if he'd just run across the continent, nodded his head. "My queen, Educator Lyshyla, you must come with me. The last bit of rock fell away in the tunnel revealing a wall of ice. We could see glimmers of blue light barely shining through. The ice has been melting since Queen Oadira arrived years ago. There's a large crack in this ice that the blue light is shining through."

Lyshyla jumped up from her seat. "There's something magical exuding a blue mist that seeps through this sheet of ice," she smiled. "We must go now!"

The four of them ran through the pyramid, out into the caverns with their crystals and shafts of light, and down the long tunnel where the work had been progressing slowly for years.

The wall of ice stood wet and thick, just as Ossa had told them, along with the crack just large enough for a person to slip through. Lyshyla went first, followed by Oadira, Ozias, and Ossa. Blue light filled the expanse, coming from a large round stone door that blocked any progress forward. Strange symbols covered the barrio, each emanating a sapphire glow, while a fire burned in the center, bright as the blue sky at midday. A pair of handprints flanked the flame, embedded into the ore itself.

"There are symbols on the tunnel door. What do they mean?" Lyshyla asked herself, stepping closer.

"Can you read them?" Oadira asked, excitement evident in her voice.

"The Nibiru tunnels can only be activated through magic and by members of the Chosen Bloodline," she translated while running her fingers along the symbols. "My queen! My king!" she shouted.

"What is it?" Oadira asked.

"It's time to leave Iceoth. The time has come," Lyshyla grinned.

"What do you mean?" Ozias questioned.

"It's all here," Lyshyla continued. "This Nibiru tunnel entrance was built by the Nibiru, those who mingled with the Kemites to help ensure that the tunnels could be built, allowing them to travel and avoid the sun."

"These tunnels kept their lives preserved so they could serve Aarde through Sahael and Egyptus looking over Alkebulan," Oadira said. "Just like we read in the nameless book that told us about the Ukáváál."

"The Nibiru were one of the first bloodlines to merge with the Kemites to help build these tunnels," Lyshyla said. "During the creation, they were built before water filled all the oceans of Aarde. Look here around the door. It's Nabopollassar's sapphire seal. It prevents the tunnel from opening. It's been built to blend in with the structure and the texture of the tunnel."

"The outside of this tunnel is outlined in aquamarine

stones," Ozias nodded. "I remember the pattern from old songs my mother would sing when I was a child. The entrance is covered in icestone, and in the center is Nile's blue flame that burns eternally to keep unwanted entries through the tunnel."

Oadira looked closer at the cerulean flame.

"This is the same flame that has kept the tunnel from collapsing and from being opened; nonetheless, this tunnel is big enough to fit several hundred people," Lyshyla said.

"Can we open the door?" Oadira asked.

"First," Lyshyla said, pointing at Ossa. "Order the people, workers, and the military to help clear out the northern section of the cavern. The debris, melting ice, and the rubble. After all the debris is removed, we'll have a clear path that'll lead the people through to the front of the tunnel entrance."

"It will take weeks to gather the people," Ozias said, looking up at the towering door.

Oadira smiled. "Then we better get started."

"Once you figure out a way to open the tunnel door, what is your plan for taking the people of Iceoth through that unopened tunnel?" Nilhist asked as he, Oadira, Ozias and Lyshyla stood on the steps of the sacred pyramid. A shaft of sunlight fell on them through an opening in the mountain, bathing them in warm light. "It's going to be a large undertaking if you are looking to leave Iceoth with all these men, women, and children. I want to be clear that I think this is a big risk you are taking."

"This is a risk that has to be attempted," Oadira said.

"These people are the lifeblood of Sahael. Without them, there is no Sahael or Sahael City. And we can't leave them behind. Eventually the colonial armies and forces of Natas will descend again, and they'll be wiped out."

"How do we know that these tunnels are intact and will work?" Nilhist asked. "I suggest that you find another way. These people were under my care for decades. A journey of this magnitude shouldn't be attempted."

"What would you have me do?" Ozias asked in frustration.

"Find another way," Nilhist replied.

"Father," Ozias said, shoulders slumping. "Come to the cavern with us. you'll see the door. We're so close."

Nilhist shook his head. "I have no wish to enter that tunnel ever, under any circumstances."

"Why not?" Oadira asked.

"My reasons are my own." Nilhist seemed to grow taller with conviction. "You can uncover the buried Nairohenge Gates by opening the door, I'm sure. But do any of you know how to use the gates? I know from my studies that without navigators and Medjay Gate Guardians, there is no way to open a portal to any specific place. We won't have any idea where we're going or how to get there. We could be lost in limbo for all time."

Lyshyla rubbed her chin in response to the former king's words. "You're right. But with the right magic..." she looked at Oadira. "And the right person, we could open the door and then use the tunnels behind it to travel to the midland of Nier's Realm and figure out how to get the people safely into Sahael from there. We do not yet understand and need answers to the events around us, and it starts with traveling to Nier's realm. I know you all have questions, and they'll be answered over time."

"You believe we can get to Neir's Realm?" Oadira asked.

"I do," Lyshyla breathed. "Because of you and Ozias. It's all becoming clear to me now. An emissary can travel there first, finding the way. Once they have done that, they can return for the rest of us."

"What are you talking about, Lyshyla?" Nilhist inquired.

She turned to Oadira and Ozias. "You remember the two sets of handprints on the door?"

"Yes," Oadira responded.

"They are for activating and removing Nabopollassar's sapphire seal," Lyshyla said. "The blood of ancients is needed to open the door. Kemettian blood is the catalyst needed to trigger and activate this Nibiru tunnel gate. From there, an emissary travels to Neir's Realm."

"Our blood?" Ozias asked.

"Yes," Lyshyla said, not mincing words. "Only your blood can activate the Nibiru tunnels. The two of you will need to cut your wrists, and when the blood begins to drip from your hands, place them on the engraved hand images to remove Nabopollassar's sapphire seal to gain access."

"Cut our wrists?" Oadira said, stepping back from Lyshyla. "Why would we do that? Why would the gods require a sacrifice like that?"

Suddenly the words Solomon had told her, Heziara and Aamira after the Royal Rumble came to mind. Her own mother had sacrificed her life to save Oadira. She had been forced to make a blood sacrifice to guarantee the protection of her daughter.

Ozias took her hand and squeezed it. "We'll do what we have to in order to protect our people."

Nodding her head, Oadira slowly agreed. "If it comes to that, yes. We will honor the sacrifices of our ancestors. If blood is required, our blood will be given. But what of our sons? If anything happens to us---"

"The boys will be protected," Nilhist nodded. "No matter the sacrifice, I will make sure those boys see their homeland."

And Oadira was satisfied. If her life was required to open the portal to Sahael, she would do it so long as she knew her children would live.

"Well," Ozias said as he entered the tunnel and waved at Oadira and Lyshyla. "It's a good thing we started the evacuation when we first found the door. Our spies have reported that colonial forces have gone out of their way to keep us from getting into Sahael. There's a Naval blockade that surrounds Iceoth, and the troops above have taken over all the cities that my father had started rebuilding. They've brought Lope Mastiffs, who have the ability to dig for miles. They know we're underground and will find this place eventually. To prevent that from happening, we must get you out of here now."

"Where are the boys?" Oadira asked.

"With Ossa. They're safe and can be brought here as soon as we're ready to go to Neir's Realm."

"How did the invaders move inland so quickly?" Oadira asked as she stepped into a puddle of water and quickly pulled her foot from the cold liquid. "It's only been two weeks since we found the door. The ships hadn't even arrived at that point."

"Blame the ice," he said with a shrug. "As spring has arrived, for the first time since our people came to Iceoth, the tundra has melted. The armies are walking on bare ground in the warm light of day. It hasn't snowed in a month.

"It should be noted that the ice started melting away the moment Oadira arrived," Lyshyla said. "This is not a new phenomenon."

"So, it's my fault?" Oadira asked, angrily. If the armies really had taken the city's remnants, they had no time to lose, and she hated thinking all of this could have been avoided if she had never come to Iceoth.

"According to the Nivenor's scrolls," Lyshyla began, placing her hand on Oadira's shoulder, "when carefully handcrafted sapphire stones interact with water, they reverse the flow of the Aarde currents. When Oadira's eyes interacted with the waters around Iceoth, the ice in the northernmost part of the caverns started melting and dripping. That's when I knew Nygaard's prophecy was true, ushering in the Signs of the Times. Look around us. Water drips from the cavern roofs like bever before. There is more water than ice down here now. Luckily, we can open the door and let the people through. We are ready."

Oadira observed all the melted ice everywhere she stepped. She had grown to love Iceoth, but the thought of finally leaving made her spirit soar. "I look forward to finally traveling to Sahael. First, we must travel to Nier's realm."

"And what happens then?" Ozias asked. "My father had a point. Without Navigators, we can't get to Sahael."

"But we can learn in Neir's Realm," Lyshyla replied. "We can train and discover how to make the gates work."

"That could take years!" Ozias shouted, voice echoing down the tunnel.

Oadira took his hand. "Husband, we need to trust Lyshyla. The Orishan Bloodline derives its divine artes, abilities, and powers, from what lies beyond Nullify's Gate in Neolithic's Chamber. Nier's realm influences every aspect of life in the sea, its color and ability to trigger life throughout Aarde. Once there, we will be safe to learn and teach. We'll find out how to travel to Sahael. It's meant to be. These are the Signs of the Times."

Word was sent for the people to gather as quickly as possible. Nilhist eventually joined Oadira, Ozias, and Lyshyla in the northernmost part of the cavern. He looked around as he entered, wiping water from his forehead that had dripped on him from above.

"I never wanted to come back here," he said with a shake of his head.

"Why not?" Ozias asked.

Nilhist paused and took a breath. "This is the tunnel where your mother died. Every day the work continued I feared I would hear news of her body being found. In the ice, all that dies is preserved. Did you find my wife's body?"

"No," Lyshyla said. "There have been no reports of any bodies found during the excavation."

"Why didn't you tell us this is where she perished?" Oadira questioned.

"Some things are better left in the mind," Nilhist replied, head bowed. "If voiced, they become real. I didn't want it to be real until the moment I needed to. If her body was not found though, what does that mean?"

"I do not know," Lyshyla said. "But our time is short. We need to open the door now and make sure we can create the gateway to Nier's Realm as the people arrive. I hear them coming even now. Holding the door open will require time and willpower. Hopefully we have enough of both."

Ozias and Oadira nodded to each other. The moment had

arrived. Their blood would be needed to open the door. Simultaneously they conjured Tetela daggers to cut their wrists. The pain of the initial cut made Oadira hesitate, but the thought of her sons surviving her possible death gave her the strength to continue. Blood gushed from the wound and Oadira instantly felt cold.

"Now, together," Lyshyla said.

Ozias, bloody hand shaking, nodded to Oadira. "Together."

They placed their bloody hands on the engraved images on the Nibiru tunnel seal. The large letter "N" lit up, causing the entire cavern to illuminate. Opal light filled the cave. Ozias's and Oadira's eyes illuminated as well, mimicking the same color as Nile's blue, cerulean flame in the center of the door.

The barrier morphed into a permeable, accessible energy field and Oadira's hand passed through it like mist.

"It's opening!" Lyshyla said excitedly. "And look!" She pointed at Oadira's wrist. "You have been healed for your faith."

Indeed, the moment Oadira's hand had passed through the translucent barrio, all pain had left her wrist. She had been healed, as had Ozias. Their faith had been rewarded.

As the light grew brighter, Oadira heard voices behind her. Turning, she saw hundreds of people led by Ossa, who walked with her three sons holding hands behind him.

The light itself seemed to become tangible in mist form, filling the cavern and touching every person within its shine.

"What's happening?" Nilhist asked.

"Look at their eyes," Lyshyla shouted. "Nile's cerulean flame is spewing out mist throughout the entire cavern."

"Their eyes are all glowing," Oadira said.

"How is this possible?" Ozias asked.

"The power of the ancients is stored within Nile's flame," Lyshyla answered. "That's why it's possible. Nile's cerulean flame was locked away according to the Sahaedron scrolls. That power has now been unleashed, igniting, and awakening the dormant gene within the bloodline of the Orishan diaspora. The Chosen Bloodline is awakening for the first time since Sahael crumbled. According to the prophesies, the people in the city of Sahaedron will be revived from death and walk Aarde once more. When that will happen no one knows, but it would be a beautiful thing to see."

Closing her eyes, Oadira felt the presence of Solomon in that moment. Words entered her mind from a voice that may have been her own or may have been that of her mentor and teacher.

The spinel mist enters the bodies of those in the cavern, eradicating the old blood within them and making them full-blooded Orishans. The spinel mist restores health to the sick and the old and extends and blesses all it touched with extended life, enabling them to live up to two hundred years. You, Oadira, have brought this miracle to your people. Be glad and follow what you know to be right.

"The Signs of the Times are upon us!" Nilhist shouted, face alight with joy.

"The Signs of the Times are upon us!" the people shouted back in unison. Tears flowed from their eyes. Children laughed. Aged old women broke into dance and song. It seemed they had all heard the voice, and all of them were filled with strength and vitality.

"What is to be done next?" Nihilist asked.

Oadira took a breath and looked at the radiant barrier before her. Beyond it she saw the Nairohenge Gates, but they were encased in icestone and rock, much like the door had been when they found it weeks before.

"The Nairohenge Gates need to be dug out of the center in the cavern to enable the people the ability to travel to Sahael once more," Lyshyla said. "The tunnel is now open to us. Now we send our emissary to find the realm."

"Who should we sand?" Ozias asked. "And how long will they be gone for?"

Lyshyla stepped through the barrier and began walking past the Gates encased in their rocky prison.

"Lyshyla!" Oadira shouted. "Where are you going?"

Turning, Lyshyla looked back with a tear in her eye. "There was only ever one emissary that could be sent. It is my journey to take. Don't worry, I will return once the path has been discovered. It will be a spiritual journey as much as a physical one. I will miss you all."

Lyshyla continued walking into the darkness beyond the Nairohenge Gates. Oadira didn't know what to do. Should she run after her? Lyshyla shouldn't travel alone.

"Let us send Ossa with you, or someone else," Oadira called. Lyshyla simply continued walking. "When will you return?"

"When my mission is completed," Lyshyla answered as she disappeared into the cavern's encompassing darkness."

Pale light continued to shine on the king, queen, their sons, and the gathered mass of people. Lyshyla had made the choice to search for their road. The rest would have to wait for her return.

"I ask again," Nilhist said, sadness in his voice. "What do we do next?"

"We wait," Oadira replied. "We wait until she returns. In the meantime, have the workers remove all the stone and ice from around the gates so when Lyshyla makes it back to us, we can be ready."

"What of the enemy forces who have captured what remain of our cities?" Nilhist asked.

Oadira looked at her husband. "Let them have them. Our people are here. We will fight when needed, but now our forces will be stronger than ever before. The colonials will weep after facing our Orishan people. Prepare them. We will return to Sahael when the gods reveal our path."

"Thy will be done, your highness," Nilhist said.

CHAPTER VI

ABILITIES, ARTES, AND POWERS

Iceoth, Pyramid, Caverns

Over the next year, the Nairohenge Gates were cleared of all stone and ice, but Lyshyla did not return. The princes grew over the year after that, learning from their mother and father, but Lyshyla did not return. Battles were fought periodically across Iceoth with both colonial forces and Onissa's Canyonland people, but Lyshyla did not return.

Eight years passed and Lyshyla still had not returned.

Even so, Queen Oadira and King Ozias shepherded their people. Colonial forces had become a constant threat. Luckily, the people of Iceoth, now stronger than ever, bathed in the power of their Orishan bloodline, were difficult to defeat and impossible to stop. Many of them had been slaves their entire lives before coming to Iceoth, and now they walked tall and proud like royalty of Sahael. Blue eyes glowed in the darkness, always eliciting fear in the hearts of the witan invaders. The ennead had not been seen in all these years, nor had the son of Natas, nor Natas himself.

Oadira wondered why, but found her time better spent in training her growing powers. Her mastery over water grew, as did her ability to transform herself.

Raising her sons took even more time and energy than worrying about her enemies or her personal training.

The boys exited their private educational classroom in the pyramid, running past their father. They were now tall and strong, 13 years of age and ready to start their combat training under the tutelage of their mother. The boys left quickly, hurrying to their training class to learn more about their magical gifts. Oadira waited on the mat for her children to sit down so she could begin their lesson. The Queen was ready to test her sons, knowing they needed to be ready before traveling through the Nibiru tunnel if Lyshyla ever came back to them.

The room they trained in was a large square with a single stone entrance. The walls were filled with water and all kinds of fish, held in place by Oadira's control over liquid. Light bounced off the water as it rippled against the air. The boys looked at the walls with amazement in their eyes.

"Are you holding the water there, Mother?" Oya asked.

"I am. Now sit."

"Yes, Mother."

"It's good that the three of you have made it on time," Oadira smiled. "There's a lot to learn, execute, and discuss today. Now that you are 13 years old, it is time for advanced training and an exam of sorts. The forces of our enemies continue to amass on our shores. You must be ready. We'll start off by learning what you are, what runs through your veins, and where your blood comes from."

Oxum, Oshún, and Oya sat down on the mat to listen to their mother speak.

"Are you ready to learn?"

"Yes, mother," the three boys nodded in unison.

"The three of you are Orishans from the Ancient and Chosen Bloodlines, two of the eight bloodlines that were combined to help create Sahael. The Chosen Bloodlines possessed abilities, allowing them to connect with the creatures of the elements. As Orisha with the blood of the chosen, we can connect with the creatures that live in the sea. We can see through their eyes, no matter where they are in Aarde. Otters, walrus, dolphins, whales, sharks, flying fish—the list goes on. Interspecies communication allows us to know all about our surroundings, seeing all and hearing all," Oadira explained.

"Can we control the creatures?" Oya asked.

"Of course, we can. Why else would they be called abilities? Duh!?" Oshún teased.

"Shut up! Before I hit you," Oya said back to Oshún.

"Quiet, sons," Oadira chided. "Keep your anger and your energies in check. Yes, Oya, we can control the animals due to the chosen power coursing through our veins. This power can be used anywhere, giving you the animal's abilities to use when needed."

Oadira hesitated to mention the other half of their abilities but knew her children needed to know.

"These abilities also allow you to shape-shift into small creatures. It's dangerous and puts you in a vulnerable position, but it can save your life in times of great need. These abilities also allow you to defy the laws of physics and do things that aren't normal for the average Orishan," Oadira said.

"What do you mean?" Oxum asked.

"What Mom means is that we can take on the form of the small creatures in the sea if we need to, but she advises against it unless we have to," Oshún said as he gave Oxum the same annoying look he gave Oya. "I've already been practicing after reading about it in the archives."

Show-off, Oya said telepathically.

At least I don't spend all my time looking at bugs, Oxum replied.

I'm studying them, Oya insisted.

Quiet, Oadira interrupted. "We will speak with our mouths, not with our minds. There is a time and place for each. Now, do any of you have questions about your Orishan abilities?" Oadira asked as she made eye contact with Oshún, Oxum, and Oya.

The three of them shook their heads left and right, indicating they had no questions.

"I've explained that you are Orisha and that we possess special abilities. The second thing I'd like to discuss with you is the Orishan artes. The Orishan artes allow you the ability to conjure up weapons of the Orisha to be used in battle, sparring, and supplying the people and our armies with their weapons."

"How?" Oshún asked. Oya and Oxum looked at him like he had asked a stupid question.

"When you blink your sapphire eyes," Oadira continued, "they activate, reflecting the color of cerulean. The veins on your palms also light up, and the image that you've thought of will appear as a weapon out of your Orishan base. I have made three of them for each of you. They consist of the symbol of Ankh. The circle is considered the uterus and inside of the uterus is the Egyptus water dragon. The image is different for each of the other three bloodlines. For the Yoruba, it's the head of an emerald short-faced bear; for the Hausa, it's an image of a hematite griffon's head; and for the Demir, it's the image of a turquoise, white rhino's head. The hilt is brown calcite with four different colored gems on each side representing the Orishan's, Yoruban's, Hausan's, and the Demirrians. The sapphire gems represent the Orisha, the emerald gems represent the Yoruba, the hematite gray gems represent the Hausa, and the turquoise gems represent the Demir. I have studied much since you were born and practiced my abilities every day in preparation for teaching you boys how to use them."

Oadira paused for a moment to allow her children to grasp the concepts of what she had just said to them. A few moments later she continued speaking.

"At the top of the hilt is Horus's Egyptus eagle with its wings spread. In the center of the eagle is the eye of Horus. The right and left wings represent something different you all should know about. The right wing represents sunrise, and the left wing represents sunset. Extending out from behind the wings are the Ankh's cross, representing Sahael and Egyptus. The last item is an image that appears through Horus's eyes that is conjured up."

"What types of images?" Oya asked.

Queen Oadira motioned for the guards to bring a weapons rack for the boys to see. The weapons rack consisted of battle axes, javelins, mace axes, Khopesh's, composite bows, spears, short swords, Konda swords, Poto Ngala swords, and Ikakalaka swords. The boys settled on the last three swords, which they were drawn to naturally. Oadira was pleased by their selections, choosing the weapons of the Orisha. After looking at the weapons, Oadira ordered that the shields be brought out so the boys could see them. The shield consisted of Nguni shields, Maasai shields, Zulu shields, Dinka shields, Mundo shields, and many others.

"The Orishan artes allow you the ability to conjure any of these weapons or shields if you choose," Oadira instructed. "Now that you've seen them, you can conjure them. The Orishan artes allow your offspring the ability to conjure up weapons on the rack and shield racks due to your bloodline abilities. The Orishan people must use normal weapons and shields that cannot be conjured up; it's special to our family's lineage."

Oadira handed the boys their Anklohs. They seemed excited to hold them as they pretended to fight against the air, swinging the swords back and forth. Oadira's heart swelled, knowing that one day they'd be fighting for their lives in a world that was in the process of being whitewashed.

"Calm down you three. I need to explain to you the last of the Orishan gifts that our bloodline possesses."

"We know most of this stuff already," Oxum said with a shrug. "And we've conjured weapons before. Grandfather has shown us many times in our training since we were five."

"Yes," Oadira replied. "But your grandfather has never placed you in a life-or-death situation. Today, that is what I'm presenting. Now, listen. When the Chosen and the Ancient Bloodlines merged, a third power was created called the Orishan power. The power to control one of the four elements was given to the Orishans from Ishtar and Obatala to watch and care for the Black inhabitants of Aarde: with the power of Hydrokinesis. To activate this power, your eyes and your tattoos will light up, enabling you to use the full scope of your powers. To activate your abilities, artes, and powers, all you have to do is blink your eyes twice, making them cerulean. This will allow you to use your Orishan gifts at your disposal."

Oshún, Oxum, and Oya all looked at each other, trying to figure out what their mother meant.

"Remember your love for each other is stronger than any of these gifts," Oadira said.

Oadira motioned for the guards to take the weapons rack and shield off the mat.

"I've explained to the three of you the powers within our bloodlines—Orishan abilities, Orishan artes, and Orishan powers. The last of the powers within our lineage is the Orishan shout. Only the high king, the great king, the king, and the regent king can perform it," Oadira said. "Now, I want the three of you to fight me using your gifts. Don't hold back because I'm not going to hold back. Blood will be spilt, but you must learn."

Oya looked at Oxum, who looked at Oshún. They didn't seem to know what to do.

"Remember," she said. "Our people were enslaved. I know you don't know what that entails, but I do. I saw it my entire life before I came to Iceoth. It is something disgusting and destructive. I never want any of you to experience anything like that, which means you will have to fight like dragons. Think quickly, respond, and attack. This may seem harsh, but I promise you boys, you will never be slaves. Your preparation is over. The battle begins now."

Oadira didn't hesitate, immediately sprinting toward Oshún using her Orishan abilities, moving faster than normal. She jumped, and connected her right foot with Oshún's chest, sending him ten feet into the air and hitting against the water-filled walls.

Queen Oadira continued the onslaught with Oshún. She used her Orishan artes, conjured up multiple spears, and hurled them at Oshún as quickly as she could.

Oshún dodged his mother's spears as they made contact with the water.

Queen Oadira continued attacking, lunging at Oshún, using her Orishan artes once more to conjure up a Nguno shield, and hitting Oshún in the back, sending him to the mat hard. As blood started dripping from his nose and mouth, scared Oxum and Oya were paralyzed, not knowing what to do.

With Oshún knocked out, Queen Oadira rushed Oxum and

Oya. Using her Orishan abilities, she forced the fish in the walls to repel light from entering the room. Queen Oadira moved around at such a speed, Oya and Oxum could barely see her.

Oadira conjured up several daggers, throwing them at her children's legs and cutting them, preventing them from moving. Oadira immediately conjured up rope, tying Oya and Oxum's legs up, throwing the rope over a beam, and hanging them both by their ankles and then moving from one side to the other, hitting them in the stomach, chest, and head each time she passed them. Groans of pain filled the room along with slight whimpers. Blood started dripping from the boys' mouths. It hit the mat, creating small puddles.

Queen Oadira then used her Orishan artes to conjure up a bow, firing at the ropes and making the boys hit the ground hard. They moaned from the beating they had just taken. In the darkness, Oadira saw her boys hit the mat with her cerulean eyes. She knew the boys hadn't activated their own abilities, so they couldn't see her. Her sons were scared, not knowing what to do as they moaned and cried in the dark.

Suddenly, the room started to brighten, and the fish were dispersed. Oshún had begun to use his Orishan abilities to communicate with the fish. Queen Oadira controlled half of the fish, and Oshún controlled the other half as they started fighting against each other in the wall tanks.

The water got bloody as Queen Oadira started winning, her half of the fish ripping Oshún's half to pieces. But then two-thirds of Queen Oadira's fish turned and started attacking what seconds before had been their allies. Oxum and Oya had joined the battle and were controlling their portion of the fish.

The numbers were now in the boys' favor.

Seeing the disadvantage, Oadira looked to change their surroundings. Closing the entrance doors, she released her hold on the water, pulling it from against the walls and filling the room.

The boys were swept off their feet and spun in the eddies now swirling around them.

Oadira stood firm, letting the water touch her skin, whispering to her of each creature beneath its depths, including her sons. The queen waited calmly before attacking, using her Orishan abilities to light up tattooed-colored gills under her ears, allowing her to breathe underwater.

The boys swam to the surface in panic, not knowing what to do.

Queen Oadira then used her Orishan power of Hydrokinesis, creating a whirlpool that forced the three brothers below the water again. As they tried to swim back to the surface for air, Oadira turned some of the water to ice, creating a cage that trapped her sons.

Her children struggled to breathe. Oadira had no desire to hurt her sons or see them suffer, but she knew they would have to adapt quickly, and it was better for them to learn the hard lessons now when their mother could still save them if needed, then letting them face men like Natas who would show no mercy. Plus, her fears of the Ukáváál had never dissipated. Should that unholy force ever enter Aard, her sons would be prepared to destroy them.

Oxum started to use his abilities to make gills appear under his ears. Oshún and Oya did the same, following his example. They were now breathing underwater effortlessly.

Good, Oadira thought. *You're seeing what I can do and adapting. Don't stop now, boys!*

But she wouldn't let up now. Oadira conjured two Ikakalaka swords, swimming at all three of her sons as if the water itself propelled her.

Oshún quickly used his Orishan artes, conjuring a Dinka

shield and Konda sword to spar with his mother. Oshún used his sword to destroy their ice prison that had trapped him and his brothers.

Queen Oadira attacked with her sword.

Oshún dodged, blocking it with his shield.

Oadira swiped at his feet.

Oshún swam up, avoiding his mother's attack.

He attempted to knee her in the face but missed as Oadira performed a back flip, avoiding Oshún's left knee. She immediately flipped forward and used her Nguni shield to knock Oshún out again.

Oxum used his Orishan artes to conjure up two Poto Ngala swords, preventing his mother from knocking him out like his brother. Oadira then moved aggressively against Oxum, charging at him and attacking relentlessly.

Oxum blocked each of his mother's attacks, but she countered everything he did to defend himself. His blocks were of no use. Seeing an opening, Queen Oadira swam down, using the base of her sword to uppercut Oxum, knocking him several feet back in the water. He spun head over feet several times before righting himself once more.

Oya slowly began to use his Orishan artes to conjure up two Konda swords as he swam over to take on his mother. Oya shook as he faced Oadira. He had always been the more sensitive and hesitant of her children, eager to please and always interested in the insects that lived in the caverns, or the birds that made their way inside from the surface. His sensitivity would serve him as a leader, but it would do nothing for him in battle.

Oadira quickly charged, sweeping his legs and forcing him to try to swim away. Spinning, Oadira kicked him in the stomach and sent him twirling toward his brothers.

The three boys, beaten and bloodied, floated together, eyeing their mother.

You two need to get up and figure something out, Oya spoke to their minds. Oadira could hear his thoughts clearly and hoped he would learn his lesson when she defeated whatever attack they believed they were planning in secret.

We're tired! Oshún said. *My nose is still bleeding.*

Mother is going to keep coming at us, Oxum replied. *It doesn't matter. The moment we take a rest, the more our asses are going to be kicked. We have to figure something out fast.*

Oya nodded. *We have to use different abilities at the same time. I will use my Orishan abilities, Oxum will use his Orishan artes, and Oshún will use his Orishan powers.*

Oadira smiled. Now they were thinking like warriors. Too bad she would beat them before they could implement any united plan.

Mother is coming! We have to be together if we are going to pose a challenge to her, Oya said.

The boys' eyes lit up cerulean, as did their tattoos—they were able to use Orishan abilities, Orishan artes, and Orishan powers, just as Oadira had hoped.

Oya used his Orishan abilities to make all of the fish inside the water-filled room circle his mother before using his Orishan abilities to move faster than usual around his mother, as the fish distracted her. Oadira countered his attack, reducing the number of fish circling her with a single mental command.

Oxum activated his Ankloh, giving him the ability to harness his Orishan artes by conjuring up a Ikakalaka sword and a Dinka shield. Oxum immediately attacked his mother who now found herself on the defensive for the first time. Oxum was able to counter all of his mother's attacks as the fish circling her, preventing her from seeing clearly.

Oshún, seeing his mother fully distracted, used his Orishan powers of Hydrokinesis to convert the water into ice. Oshún's tattoos lit up brightly as he created a large, thick cage with the top closed to prevent his mother from exiting once it was placed on top of her.

Oshún, Oxum, and Oya were now working together as their minds synced up with each other, using their Orishan powers to communicate telepathically. The three brothers moved as one as they fought against their mother. Oadira tried to swim and avoid becoming trapped, but she wasn't fast enough as Oshún dropped the cage on his mother.

Oadira could feel the connection between her sons. Pride swelled in her heart and for a moment she considered ending the training session so they could feel proud of their win. Pride wouldn't keep them from becoming slaves though, so she persisted. Using her Orishan powers, Oadira destroyed the ice cage. The force blew the boys up and out of the water, splashing back down like limp rags.

The entry door opened, and the water began emptying from the room. The boys coughed as they lay on the wet stone floor, fish flopping around them.

"Well done!" Oadira beamed. "After several years of training, the three of you have passed the Orisha training exam. Class is dismissed."

"But we lost," Oya coughed.

"Victory was never the point," a voice echoed from the back of the room. Ozias stepped through the entrance, boots splashing in the puddles left behind by the receding flood. "This was part one of your three Orishan exams. Your mother showed you no mercy, knowing that if she did, you'd be killed in the real world. It may not seem like it, but your mother has prepared the three of you for whatever you will face. I'm happy she's done so. You were never going to beat her. You needed to show you could adapt, work as a team, and think quickly, which you did."

The boys quickly hugged their mother, showing their love for her.

"I'm sorry, but it had to be done," Oadira said, breaking the embrace. "If it was your father, you may have beaten him, but not me. and I held back. Remember, the witans will treat you terribly due to the color of your skin, and they will show no mercy. I have no doubts that the three of you are ready to deal with what Aarde will throw at you, if your father and I aren't around to protect you." Sapphire tears ran down her ebony checks.

Ozias smiled. "I don't know if you could have beaten me, but I'll defer to your mother's knowledge on that one. The three of you will be ready when the time comes, and the people will follow any and all of you as their leaders."

"The ability to control your artes and powers is rare and an accomplishment you should be proud of," Oadira said, picking up a fish and throwing it into a deeper puddle so it wouldn't suffocate. "According to many of the pyramid records, before the fall of Sahael, many of the ancient-blooded families had sons and daughters who were unable to pass the Orishan exam."

"What happened to them?" Oshún asked.

"They were sent to the Society of Secrets. Many children of the four bloodlines who were born out of wedlock were sent there as well, unless they passed the Orishan trials and were permitted to join their family bloodline."

"The Society of Secrets?" Oxum questioned.

"They're a group of spies that work for the royal lineages of Sahael," Oadira answered.

"What did they do for Sahael?" Oshún asked, clearly keen on wanting to know more about them.

Oadira grinned and motioned for her sons and husband to follow her. They walked through the halls of the pyramid archives toward the exit.

"The Society of Secrets," she began, "watches over the four bloodlines in Sahael and the Kemetic bloodline in Egyptus, always staying in the shadows. Their purpose is to look out for any members who share the Ancient Bloodline anywhere in Aarde. They did this to make sure that if any of the royal bloodlines in Sahael were eradicated, they'd know where to find any of the remnants hiding in Aarde."

"Where are they now?" Oshún asked.

"Hidden in the shadows. Only those who are a part of their order know where they live. After the fall of Sahael, their order was to be hunted and a command was issued by the pharaohs and the Ptolemies of Egyptus through Vizier Hemiunu."

"What did they do to be hunted by our people? Weren't they the good guys?" Oya asked, now seemingly as interested as his brother.

The group exited the pyramid, stepping into the primary cavern with its glowing crystal formations and forested landscape. Even though they were underground, it still seemed as if the sun shone above them on this breezy afternoon.

"The society betrayed the people of Sahael," Oadira answered as they descended the steps toward the waving grasses and the gardeners picking swamp flowers. "They helped Lord Commander Natas infiltrate Sahael by providing everything he wanted to know about the four bloodlines in Sahaerion, Sahaedeath, Sahaeland, and Sahaedron, The Society of Secrets gave the lord commander intel about the comings and goings of what was happening inside of Khartoum Palace."

"They helped destroy Sahael?" Oxum asked, balling his fists.

"It looks that way," Oadira nodded.

"Why?"

"I don't know. I'd like to find out the reasons that may have led them to do what they did. There are always two sides to a story. They'll one day have to explain their reasoning as to why they betrayed their people. Lyshyla taught me many of the more recent happenings that aren't in the archive before she left for Neir's Realm many years ago. There are still things I don't know the answer to. Perhaps one day we can all learn them together. Now go, my sons. Enjoy the rest of the day with your friends."

"Can we go up to the surface?" Oya asked. "There is still ice in some of the crevasses, and I would like to look at the roaches that breed there."

"Yeah!" Oxum added. "And we can jump from the cliff there into the drifts with Nelhax and Romul."

"Just be careful!" Oadira shouted as the boys ran off. "And don't get in trouble up there. Nelhax is a bad influence on you!"

Ozias put his arm around Oadira's waist and pulled her close to him. "You sound like Lyshyla as you teach the boys. It's like you're the Educator now, spinning tales of history for all to hear."

"I've learned all I can here," Oadira said, snuggling into her husband's shoulder. "Over the years, I've read every book in the library. Maybe one day I'll get to travel to Timbuktu and learn all the knowledge in existence. That would be wonderful."

The king and queen stood there at the bottom of the pyramid steps, feeling the wind blow on their faces. The smells of sweet grass and decaying plants tickled their senses.

Just then, Ossa came running out of the trees toward them. He smiled broadly.

"Your highness!" he shouted. "Your highness!"

"What it, Ossa?" Ozias asked as the man approached, out of breath. "You look like you've run from a stampede of mammoths."

"I bring word from the tunnels. There is much rejoicing."

Oadira's forehead wrinkled over her brow. "What's going on?"

"Lyshyla has returned!"

CHAPTER VII

THE NIBIRU TUNNELS

The Nibiru Tunnels

By nightfall, word had spread to all the people that after eight years, Lyshyla had emerged from Nibiru's Tunnel. She wore a pale white robe with a silver belt and accents, but other than that, she looked exactly the same as when she had left so long ago. That evening she told Ozias and Oadira about her travels, and that she had found Nier's Realm fairly quickly, following her own insights and the prompting she felt from the gods. Once there, she knew she couldn't return right away. There was much for her to learn, and she realized the people would not be ready to leave Iceoth until the royal princes were able to defend themselves.

"I knew my time was close," Lyshyla said as she drank warm Amarula in the sitting area of the archive where she, Oadira and Ozias had spent so much time after Oadira had first arrived in Iceoth. "I felt compelled to return, knowing your sons were ready to travel to the realm. From what you tell me, the boys have demonstrated they can take care of themselves, so that's one less thing to worry about."

"It's so good to have you back," Ozias beamed.

"What is Neir's Realm like?" Oadira asked. "I've been wondering for eight years!"

"It's lovely," Lyshyla smiled. "You'll see it soon enough. The time has come, and word needs to be sent out. Our people will be traveling within the week. Food will need to be gathered, supplies of all types. I know the path, so we will not wander."

"My father will be very happy to see you when he returns from his patrols tomorrow," Ozias mentioned.

"I'm sure he will," Lyshyla said, drinking the rest of her Amarula. "Ozias, would you mind bringing me some more dried mammoth meat? I am still very hungry."

"Of course." Ozias jumped up and left the room in search of more food.

"Traveling north will not be easy," Lyshyla said, placing her hand on top of Oadira's. "The fact your sons can take care of themselves is less stress on all of us, especially you, since you are expecting another child."

"What!?" Queen Oadira said, eyes wide. "How do you know that?"

"Look at you! Your skin, your eyes—you're radiating," Lyshyla said. "Even before my time in Neir's Realm I could tell when a woman was pregnant before she could. This is a blessing that I'm glad I didn't miss."

"This isn't good," Oadira said, sitting up straighter and rubbing her stomach. "If Ozias finds out, he'll want to wait to leave until after the baby is born."

"So, what do you want to do?" Lyshyla asked.

"I'll tell the king after we've already left." Queen Oadira said.

Lyshyla nodded her head in agreement.

Over the next several days, the royal family prepared for their long trip north. Queen Oadira helped get the boys prepared as they continued to practice their abilities, artes, and powers. Nilhist helped with the preparations, ensuring they would have all they needed. King Ozias ordered a small cohort of Anubis troops and a large percentage of the Orishan peoples to help with the preparations as they traveled with them through the tunnels. The royal family didn't want to give away any clues they were leaving; they wanted to avoid having a scout hear them from above, revealing their location. As the ice had melted over the years, more and more of the entry tunnels had been discovered by Colonial troops. Only through much fighting and vigilance had the cavern's location remained a secret.

As night approached, the conclave entered the tunnel. Several thousand people would be traveling with the royal family and military force, while Nilhist remained behind as planned to rule Iceoth's remaining population, once again as its king.

Nilhist agreed to accompany his son's family for a short time before saying goodbye.

The Nibiru tunnels were underground passageways dug throughout Aarde and built beneath the land and under the sea. They were enclosed except for the entrances and exits at each end. Pale lights emanated at intervals, glowing blue. Bioluminescent insects crawled here and there like scurrying lanterns, much to the excitement of Oya.

"The sapphire stones you see dotted all over these tunnels are lit up in various colors to provide us with light," Lyshyla pointed out to everyone.

"Where do the lights lead?" Oadira asked.

"To various locations all over Aarde, the four realms, and every island in Aarde," Lyshyla said. "As you can see, the tunnels are expansive. Finding Neir's Realm was not easy, but now I know the way quite well."

"Can we get to all of these locations just from the tunnels?" Ozias asked.

"Yes," Lyshyla said. "This is the only one to get to Iceoth besides the ocean that I'm aware of. After Sahael fell, information was no longer accessible. Many thought this tunnel gate to Iceoth got destroyed by Nygaard to prevent any threats from entering Iceoth and to protect the people and cut off all contact with Sahael."

Ozias turned to Nilhist. "Father, you insisted that it was to preserve the Ancient Bloodline, knowing that one day Nygaard's prophecy would be fulfilled."

"Agreed, but orders were given to me to destroy this Nibiru tunnel," Nilhist said as he walked beside his grandsons. "Your mother prevented me from knowing the tunnel's importance for reasons beyond my understanding. As a result, she gave her life to put Nabopollassar's seal on the tunnel. Her sacrifice protected the cavern and saved the people from being destroyed. To this day, I wish we had found her body in the caverns. It was crushed and destroyed over the years, no doubt. I simply wish we could have buried her. I wish she were by my side even now. I'll continue protecting the people as long as I live." Nilhist embraced his only son. "Farewell, Ozias Ocnus, my son. May we meet again on the shores of Sahael. Until then, may Iceoth always be considered your home. You will be protected here, as will your family. Until our next meeting in the sun of a bright winter morning! *Familie moet uitkyk vir familie,"* he said as he walked away, leaving them at a fork in the tunnel.

"He is not the same man that I met all those years ago, sitting on his throne and despising the refugees," Oadira smiled.

"No, he is not," Ozias agreed. "He's going back to protect new refugees coming in from Lucedale who need his help so that they'll be able to get to Sahael eventually. Now that Nile's flame is lit, those entering the cavern will have their eyes and years restored, allowing them to be young once again. After having their years taken away from them through enslavement, they'll be given back to them. Afterward, Nilhist will make sure they travel through the tunnels with the Anubis warriors stationed along the way. I pray I can be as good a leader as him as my own years progress."

"You will," Oadira confirmed with a kiss.

Over the next few days, the group traveled through the darkness, never knowing whether it was morning or evening. Lyshyla had them rest at specific intervals, eyes always on the path forward. The glowing rocks provided just enough light to travel, but darkness seemed ever present, pushing in on them with each step.

"Traveling through this tunnel should be done as quickly as possible," Oadira said on the fourth day. "I worry about the children, so I'll keep a close eye on them as we travel through each section of the tunnels."

"My eyes are having difficulty adjusting," Ozias said.

Oshún, Oxum, and Oya complained they couldn't see at all and started bugging each other to eat up time.

"These stones respond to touch. If you touch them, they light up more brightly," Lyshyla informed. "There are five different types of colored lights at the tops of the tunnels every fifteen feet built by the Nibiru. The five differently colored stones represent the four bloodlines of Sahael; these tunnels were derived from the center of Khartoum Palace. The Nibiru retrofitted them for the ancient lineages and for themselves, to help build more tunnels. The diamonds, when activated, provide light in general to the tunnel."

"Okay, I'll try touching the clear stones and the sapphire stones," Ozias said. He touched the stones, but nothing happened.

"Perhaps if you and your wife touch them, they might light up, allowing everyone around us to see through the tunnel," Lyshyla suggested.

"If it provides more light, I say we should do it," Oadira said.

Oadira and Ozias touched the stones, and shortly thereafter, the diamond stones and the sapphires stones lit up, illuminating the tunnels. While still dark, at least the walls of the cave were easier to make out. Fewer people stumbled behind them.

Another day passed. The group approached a large, six-way opening with multiple doors opening the moment they arrived. Each door had the symbol of a large helmet with the letter "N" in the center of it symbolizing the Nibiru, a mark they left on everything they built inside of the tunnels. The area looked to be where a lot of traffic once happened, and people interacted with each other. Remnants of old shops and carts littered the ground.

"This looks like a good place to rest," Oadira said as she sat down with her sons.

"How are you holding up?" Ozias asked.

"This whole thing is overwhelming," Oadira said.

"The fear of failing is written all over your heart. I can feel it," Ozias said as he wrapped his arms around her. "I'll have the guards make camp and put the boys in their own tent. Are you okay? You seem to be walking extra carefully."

"I'm…" Oadira began. "…fine."

For a moment she considered telling him she was pregnant but knew he would be even more worried about dangers than she was. It was best to get through the tunnel before that blessed news added weight to her husband's shoulders.

After Ozias had put the boys in their own tent, he and his wife looked at their children. "Everything will be all right," Ozias said, whispering in her ear. "We'll get through this together," he said to her as they both lied down and nestled on the hard ground beneath warm blankets.

Somewhere in the deep of the night, Oadira heard a shout. She sat up, as did Ozias.

"What was that?" he asked.

"It sounded like Oya!"

The king and queen jumped from their canvas tent and looked into the darkness. Oadira activated her dark sight and saw her three sons fighting what looked like a giant spider the size of large man. Oadira ran forward, leaving her husband in the dark as he shouted after her, terrified her sons had been hurt. As she approached though, she realized the boys were laughing.

"You're covered in its blood!" Oxum giggled.

"We killed it!" Oshún shouted.

Oadira rushed to her children's side. "What are you doing?!" she cried. "You're supposed to be sleeping."

"We're okay," Oya said, completely covered from head to toe in red goo as he crawled out from under the dead creature. "We found a Treep nest while we were---"

"Shut up, Oya!" Oxum said. "You're gonna get us in trouble."

"She knows we go out of our tent, Oxum," Oshún said as

he slugged his brother in the arm. "Besides, we killed it."

"Mother, we were amazing!" Oya gushed. "We worked together and---"

"Boys!" Ozias shouted as he approached in the darkness. 'What are you doing? We don't know the dangers of these caves, and Lyshyla told everyone to avoid wandering off."

"We found a Treep nest by accident," Oya repeated. "We snuck outside of the camp and fell down a tunnel and encountered some large spiders. One of the big ones followed us out and tried to web us up, but it's dead now."

The Treep's body started to convulse with a sickening sloshing sound.

"Treeps aren't so easily disposed of, boys," Ozias said angrily.

The princes watched in horrific anticipation as the body violently shuddered and tore open, releasing hundreds of smaller Treep's the size of rats. The mountain of bioluminescent creatures clamored over each other, sprinting back into the tunnels away from the camp.

"We have to get back to camp and warn Lyshyla! It's time to get out of this tunnel!" Oadira said.

The family sprinted back through the darkness, practically running into Lyshyla as she walked toward them.

"What happened?" Lyshyla asked.

"We killed one of them," Oxum said so fast his words blended together. "and it broke off and made more of these little spiders and retreated into the darkness of the tunnels!"

"Then they started to follow us. We hurried back to camp to warn you," Oshún said as he caught his breath.

"How many times have we told you not to run off?"

Lyshyla said, upset. "Well at least now I know why our camp is being assaulted. My king, my queen, trouble is approaching, and the guards have all been placed on notice. Moments ago, a group of Treeps tried to carry away some of the people resting on the edge of our group. They were massive, far larger than anything I've ever seen in the tunnels. Within minutes we could be overrun by thousands of them. Danger is approaching! Prepare to defend the people!"

A bell rang, notifying everyone of incoming danger. Anubis warriors ran this way and that, while sleeping people awoke with a start.

Oadira blinked her eyes twice, activating her Orishan gifts and conjuring weapons as she walked around the perimeter of the camp.

"Everyone has been alerted," Lyshyla said, running up to the king and queen. "With the nest disturbed, we should try and reach the surface. There are tunnels that make their way to the surface of the sea in this area. If we can get there, we can drown the Treeps. Otherwise, we could potentially lose hundreds of people to the spiders. Better to risk the water than die inside these tunnels."

"Everyone needs to leave as soon as possible to prepare the people to follow," Ozias ordered.

The Orishan people frantically hurried down a narrow pathway, led by Lyshyla.

Oadira mingled with the people, shouting orders and trying to keep the people calm. Every now and then shouts would rise up as Treeps invaded the throng, trying to bite and carry away whomever they could.

"I want to make sure we don't lose anyone," Oadira shouted to Ozias, who led the group with Lyshyla and the boys.

"I'll protect the rear from these creatures. I can sense a weakness in the spiders."

Oadira, along with a group of her Orishan people, fought against the invading spiders. Oadira sliced two Treeps from head to thorax while several others were killed with stones by the courageous civilians. Just as expected, rat-like, bioluminescent spiders came out of each dead Treep's body. The arachnids didn't retreat this time, swarming forward with larger beasts behind them. Even the small Treeps were a danger as they spit venom at their targets. The bigger ones, easily bigger than the largest Orishan, shot webs from their spinnerets in an attempt to trip fleeing targets.

Oadira conjured darts, picking the small creatures off one by one with an energetic blowgun. Still, the rat-like Treeps lunged toward the queen with ferocious tenacity.

"Fine, I'll use daggers and kill you ugly things," Oadira shouted. She jumped in the air, spinning and contorting her body, conjuring up whips in both of her hands, slashing and slicing hundreds of Treeps. This act killed the rat-like Treeps that had joined in a coordinated attack against her. But more Treeps emerged from the cracks.

The second wave of rat-like Treeps came at her as the people screamed. The queen looked toward the clamoring spiders as they climbed on the sides and ceiling of the tunnel.

"They're attacking the people and dragging them away from the group," Ozias shouted. "They've taken out nearly all the Anubis warriors."

"I'll save those that I can," Lyshyla said, running toward Oadira.

"Boys, it's time to do your part to help save your people," Oadira said. "You started this with your foolishness. Now you need to help us finish it!"

Focused and determined, her boys rushed to her side, manifesting weapons as they ran. Oshún protected from the front, Oxum and Oya were on the right side, and Lyshyla took up the left. Oadira made her way to the back where Ozias protected the rim. They fought valiantly alongside their sons, cutting down Treeps left and right, but for every one they killed, it seemed a hundred took its place.

"I have to stay here to make sure no other Treeps are coming up the rear. I will stay and protect everyone," Ozias yelled.

The Treeps continued moving faster, breaking through their lines, and killing more people with each wave of attack. Every oversized spider that fell, exploded, and spit out a hundred smaller versions that bit and swarmed with a ferocity that terrified Oadira. One Treep got close enough to lunge toward her from a crevice in the tunnel. Oadira blinked her eyes twice, activating her Orishan gifts, and conjured an Orishan long spear, throwing it toward the ceiling and impaling the Treep on it, killing it instantly.

"We need to figure something out fast, or we're all going to die in these tunnels. I have an idea," Ozias said.

"What's your idea?" Oadira asked.

"Can you communicate with them using your Orishan abilities?" Ozias asked.

"There's too many. We'll both have to do it," Oadira suggested.

"Then let's do it," Ozias said,

They both placed their hands on the closest injured Treep, looking through the creature's mind and communicating with the other attacking arachnids. They all paused suddenly, retreating for a moment into the darkness. The people and children looked on as their cerulean glow illuminated the space along with Lyshyla's lavender eyes.

"We must kill them all as soon as we release our hold. They'll regroup and come for us once again," Oadira said.

"I'll draw the Treep's away while everyone can get to the surface safely," Ozias said.

"No! I won't separate my family under any circumstances. We'll stay together at all costs!" Oadira said.

Oadira wasn't willing to risk any family members; she didn't want to experience the pain of what she had to go through when she was a little girl.

"I must tell you that by the blessings of Ibeji, we are expecting our fourth child," she admitted, grasping Ozias' hands. "I refuse to have our family separated no matter the circumstances."

Ozias looked at his wife, solemn and silent. He hugged her and kissed her on the forehead.

"I'm not going anywhere," he said with a smile. "After all, I have another child to meet!"

"We'll all arrive at our destination together," Oadira said.

"Then we'll go down another path," Ozias said. "Lyshyla! Where are we going?"

"This path may lead us to open water," Lyshyla answered. Webs stuck in her head and a line of blood ran from her hairline. "We'll have to exit from a swimming point and swim the rest of the way. To do this, we'll need to step out of Nabopollassar's seal, which protects the integrity of the tunnels and allows the water not to flood the caverns. If you remove Nabopollassar's seal, it would wipe out the Treep's, killing them all and their young."

"We'll drown!" someone shouted from the crowd.

"I've never swum before," yelled another.

The people instantly grew fearful. Oadira could feel the

emotions as they rippled through the gathering. Panic set in, and the overlapped chatter of growing concerns became loud as the Treeps returned, moving in closer to them once again. Oadira whistled loudly, hushing the population.

"What do you all have to fear?" she shouted. "Are you not of the Orishan bloodline? Does Orishan blood not flow through your veins? Who are your ancestors? Do not forget who you are!"

The people listened as Oadira spoke.

"Our ancestors have survived far worse than what lies before us," she continued, voice echoing through the tunnel. "Every one of us has the inherent ability to live through this ordeal! Remember the attack of the colonial army in the clearing! Remember our victory! Remember the years since, as we have protected each other and been blessed with power and long life because of it. The water you are afraid of is our life source! We are one with it and can use it to our advantage. You shall not fear the element that gives you life, gives you purpose, and gives you power! Use that power to save yourselves, and the people of Sahael!"

Oadira, using her Orishan powers, reactivated the people's natural gifts by waving her left hand over the people. As she did so, three lines appeared in cerulean under the earlobes of the people, allowing them to breathe under water.

"We are all going to run as quickly as we can to keep the distance between us and the Treep's until we get to one of the open waters exits," Ozias said to everyone. "you can breathe under water now, so don't fear."

Oadira led her people forward along the tunnel, hearing the Treeps gaining on them from behind. Despite her brave words, Oadira knew if they didn't reach the barrier soon, they would be overrun by spiders. If that happened, the last great flight of the Orishan people would never be remembered by any living soul in

Aarde, as they would all be corpses by morning.

[To be continued on Volume 1 Book 4]

OUT NOW:

VOLUME ONE

BOOK FOUR

ANCIENT REMNANTS

Made in the USA
Columbia, SC
25 May 2024

d62df294-7a33-4f42-b36a-84bbff587f92R01